A Thrill
A Minute

By

David O'Neil

Argus Enterprises International, Inc.
New Jersey***North Carolina

A Thrill A Minute © 2013 All rights reserved by David O'Neil

A-Argus Better Book Publishers, LLC

For information: A-Argus Better Book Publishers, LLC
9001 Ridge Hill Street
Kernersville, North Carolina 27285
www.a-argusbooks.com

ISBN: 978-0-6157770-0-9
ISBN: 0-6157770-0-7

Book Cover designed by Dubya

Printed in the United States of America

Chapter one

Hurrying down the corridor, Abby Marshall was not really looking where she was going. The collision occurred and the bag she was carrying slid across the floor, closely followed by the young man who had backed into her. He was sprawled out on the corridor floor looking scared, feet already scrabbling for grip to get back on his feet and running.

Abby looked down the side corridor he had emerged from. She saw the back of a tall man, with a dirty blond ponytail, blue jean shirt and black chinos, disappearing around the corner at the far end.

Picking up her bag, she turned to the fallen man to find that he had also gone. *No apology, nothing?* She shrugged and resumed her interrupted journey to the lecture she was due to attend.

Abby Marshal and Donny Weston had been together now for nearly four years, though only now engaged formally. Since they had been in High School, from the age of sixteen they had spent most of the time in each other's company.

It had been an eventful time for them both, and on several occasions during that period they had been close to being killed. Quick reactions and quick thinking had saved them both on several occasions since the first attempt to dispose of them on a cruise to France. Then an accidental spilling of Donny's drink had made the difference between life and death for them both. *

Since then the pair had been inseparable. The bond between them had strengthened with every subsequent attempt to remove them, and their own efforts to survive.

For the past eighteen months both had been able to return to the studies they had interrupted after their latest skirmish with trouble.

After three excursions into Europe and a trip to USA, they had put the threats to their lives behind them. Both were now studying for degrees in Law at Brunel University, Uxbridge, to the west of London.

Abby and her fiancé, Donny Weston, linked-up to share the ride home to their apartment in Hillingdon, four miles away from campus. Seated in their Citroen 2CV, on the way Abby commented on the incident in the corridor.

Donny said. "Interesting. One of the Polish students in my English literature group was late for the lecture. He arrived looking really hassled. In fact the old 'Grouse' was actually quite nice to

*See Fatal Meeting

him. Professor Moor PHD, known as 'Old Grouse' suggested that, whilst being late was wrong, he should not get too worried provided it did not become a habit.

"I was thinking that it was unlikely that Pavel, (that's the student's name,) was too worried about being late. Whatever upset him was obviously something much more serious. The door was opened a couple of times during the lecture, and each time he looked ready to run out of the other door."

Abby said. "I did not recognize the man with the ponytail. I'm sure he was something to do with Pavel's panic."

Donny thought for a minute. "I know him. At least I think I do. He hangs around a lot with Anson Canvan, you know, the guy who came on to you at the Student Ball last year?"

"You mean that creep who tried to grope me while I was talking to Annabelle Arden, the QC?"

Donny looked puzzled. "Annabel who?"

Abby said impatiently, "The visiting Law lecturer!" She continued. "I remember him now. He sprained his little finger when he touched my leg. He didn't dare comment or even cry out with Annabelle standing there ready to witness and

perhaps give evidence. I meant to tell you about it but it must have slipped my mind."

"You say he sprained his little finger touching your leg?"

"Yes, my hand was there at the same time. I could have actually broken it. Guys like that need to learn to keep their hands to themselves." She shrugged. "All the fuss and bother that would have caused? I decided it wasn't worth it, so I sprained it instead."

At home later that evening, they were both in the kitchen of the apartment. Abby was chopping salad, Donny, peeling potatoes. smiled to himself as he recalled the story of Canvan having a sprained finger from trying to grope Abby. He had been a lucky man. The last one to try that on Abby died in Las Vegas. Of course there had been other reasons as well.

He carried on with cooking the potatoes. After a year and a half sharing the apartment, they had the routine down between them. Both were good cooks, and on occasion, each would take a turn producing the meal. Otherwise they shared the chores.

Selecting another tomato, Abby asked, "You mentioned the creep that tried to grope me, Canvan somebody. Who is he? Why does the name ring a bell somewhere in the back of my mind?"

"Anson Canvan is, not surprising, the son of Michael Canvan the Member of Parliament, former CEO of Canvan Industries, though now apparently separated from the business. He is a multi-millionaire, owns houses all over the place, in the world that is. His three million pound yacht is moored in the Hamble somewhere. The son Anson Canvan is the arrogant piece of work who drives the Orange Lamborghini that is regularly parked at Brunel?"

"Oh, that Canvan." She thought for a moment. "Didn't I hear something about insider trading associated with that name?"

"That was Anson's cousin. He was found guilty of insider trading, convicted and sent away for four years. if I remember correctly."

"Didn't he plead that he was briefed and ordered to do the trade in question by Michael Canvan?"

"He did, but it was denied successfully by Michael. Nobody could prove that he had actually benefitted financially because the money trail was lost before the illegal trade was exposed."

"In prison you say, so much for family ties!"

"In company with people friendly to the man who put him there. I noticed that he had suffered several injuries from 'accidents' that indicate that he must be the most accident prone inmate in that particular establishment."

"I wonder if Jonathon would know anything about this man." Abby was intrigued.

Donny looked at her sharply. "Are you finding life within these hallowed walls boring perhaps?"

"It's odd that you should say that. Up to now, I genuinely don't think I was. But now I wonder? I have the feeling that Canvan and his associates will be bad news."

Donny quoted in a sepulchral voice, "I can tell by the pricking of my thumbs, something wicked this way comes!"

Abby waved the chopping knife at him. "Don't mock. I have been right before about things like this, and you know it."

Donny laughed and held up his hands in surrender. "Okay, I agree I think there may well be something going on involving Canvan. He is a nasty piece of work as you say."

The telephone rang, interrupting the discussion at that point.

Abby lifted the receiver, and looking at the caller ID said, "Hullo, Jonathon." She listened for a moment, and then she said, "I'll stick another spud in the pot; see you shortly. Bye"

Turning to Donny, she said, "That was spooky. Jonathon is in the area and asks if he can drop in for a drink. That means he will probably stay for dinner."

Donny looked at her, a tight smile on his face. "Jonathon never 'just' drops in anywhere!"

Abby shrugged, and turned to finish off the preparation of the salad.

***

The Orange Lamborghini stood outside the large house in Cowley. Lying as it did at the halfway point between Uxbridge and Hounslow, the village had largely succumbed to the urban encroachment that had been creeping outward over the past twenty years. The current, ever-increasing demand for accommodation created by the expansion of London Airport was now eroding the farmland that had traditionally been the feature of the area.

In Cowley, there were still houses remaining in the areas backing onto the surviving green fields that still existed around the village.

Cornmill House was surrounded by two acres of garden. The gravel drive was raked and the lawn cut regularly. The staff ran the house with the quiet efficiency typical of the country houses of a past age. They were well paid for their work, and all were aware that their jobs depended on maintaining that atmosphere.

Anson Canvan sat in the drawing room facing his father, with a scotch in his hand. He hefted the heavy crystal tumbler and took a sip.

The smooth 12-year-old, single malt slipped down easily as he listened to his father.

"It will be necessary for me to take a holiday for a month or so. Jarvis, the accountant will look after the finances in the meanwhile. Walker runs the business, so you will have no problems to deal with, there. I will remain in contact with him wherever I am. Have you got that?"

"Yes, father. As you have pointed out already, I will just get on with my studies while your hard men carry on with their illegal activities."

Michael Canvan looked at his son with disgust. "Don't you dare talk to me like that. Those, so-called activities have paid for you motor, clothes and your education, so don't get smart with me. You benefit from the family business, and always have. In my day I lived in a single room in the Gorbals, in Glasgow. I grew up with the scent of piss and shit from the common toilet down the hall. All you know about is a posh room with an en-suite bathroom, clean sheets, and fresh clothing with designer labels. You drive a car that would have bought the entire street where I was brought up and given more change than I earned in the first ten years of my working life."

"All right, father. I've got the message. I am grateful!" Anson was sick of hearing it. Each little incident brought out the same old lecture.

That stupid thirteen-year-old that got herself pregnant and had to be bought-off was the last time. The fact that it was the latest of many such feckless incidents had never occurred to him, and apparently never would.

He resented his father, especially when he found out about his father's real business, or at least a major part of his real business. If his father had allowed him to choose one or two of the girls his business imported illegally, the fact that they were brought in against their will would have made things even better from Anson's point of view.

Having mentioned it on the one occasion, Anson never dared bring the matter up again. His father had been furious and had scared Anson half to death. The imported girls came in by the dozen. His father maintained that a good looking virgin was worth thousands to him; it was a matter of business. He had pointed out that there were plenty of women here in Britain ready to give it away free, just don't pick on thirteen year olds in future.

His departure was unannounced and timed to evade any awkward questions that may have been difficult to answer at that particular moment.

Despite the sensible advice from his father and although Anson liked older women and played games with them when the opportunity offered, he really preferred the younger edition. Now with his father away in Bermuda, Anson was feeling his feet. Particularly since the reason his father was travelling was an urgent request from the police to come and chat. He decided that since his father would not be returning for some considerable time, the responsibility for the business must of necessity fall on his shoulders. His first tentative attempts in taking control brought him in direct conflict with his father's deputy, who in turn was under instruction, by internet, from Canvan senior.

Almost incoherent with frustration and sheer temper he strode through the corridors of the University, daring anyone to stand in his way. He felt his day was complete when he and his pony-tailed follower encountered Abby and a girlfriend chatting in his direct path.

"Move!" he shouted at the two women, "Get out of the way!"

Abby's companion made to move to the wall, Abby stopped her and turned round to face the angry figure bearing down on them. Looking directly at him she said with a smile, "Move yourself!" She ordered in a deceptively quiet voice.

Anson gestured to his companion to sweep the two women aside. The impact made by his falling companion knocked him off his feet to hit the ground with a painful impact, causing him to scrape his arm painfully on the floor.

Without thinking he sprang to his feet and lashed out at the bloody woman.

With a painful wrench he hit the floor once more. His companion was back on his feet in a crouch stalking Abby who was just standing looking relaxed. As pony-tail leaped forward Abby kicked him in the knee with the toe of her boot. He crumpled to the floor alongside his boss, clutching his knee in agony.

"Come, Sally," Abby called to her friend. "The smell here would insult a pig. Let's find somewhere more agreeable to have our chat."

Anson Canvan was incoherent with rage. He was beside himself. He had been treated like an irritating fly—by a woman. And she had brushed off his bodyguard as if he was nothing. Having seen his bodyguard, Crilley, deal with three hard men at once, it only made it harder to believe. As he continued his interrupted journey dark thoughts of revenge, entailing the ripping off of clothing, beating bare skin and savage sexual reprisal, crossed and re-crossed his mind.

Abby and Sally met up with Donny after their next class,

"I had a run in with Anson Canvan earlier this afternoon." Abby said.

"I heard all about it. It must be all over the University by now. I'm told the idiot asked for it, and you were just the one to serve it out." He grinned. "I guess they were surprised, Crilley especially."

"You could say that!" Sally said. "I was stunned. One moment the two arseholes were bearing down on us like gangbusters. They were shedding people right and left from their path, whether they liked it or not. Then Abby put me to one side and wham! Bang! Crilley is going backward into Anson, both hit the floor. Anson got up and took a swing at Abby, who flattened him once more. Crilley crept round to get at Abby, so she kicked him in the knee and he finished up beside his boss on the floor again hugging his knee." She laughed. "They really did not know what hit them."

During the journey home, Donny referred to the visit made by their friend, Jonathon Glynn, several days ago. Since then there had been two chatty phone calls from the same source. Jonathon Glynn was a member of the security services and had been a factor in both the origin and the successful conclusion of the events of the past three years. The suspicions inspired by Jonathon's latest contact had been confirmed after the latest phone call.

"Social visit, my ass. Jonathon drops in casually. Mentions the fact that daddy Canvan might be less than lily-white. Oh, yes. I believe his son attends the Business Management course at Brunel. Have you come across him?" He paused and drew up at traffic lights. "Now, I understand, daddy has gone abroad, one jump ahead of an enquiring policeman. Why do I get the feeling that we are being set up for something?"

Abby smiled. "Well, I for one was getting a little restless. If I know you as well as I think I do, so are you. After all it's been a while since we last saw action, and much though I enjoy being here in this most interesting place, there are times when it gets a trifle tedious."

Donny thought about things for a few moments. "From what Jonathon was saying, I have the impression that the investigation he is carrying out is involved with drugs and the illegal importation of slaves from the former Eastern European countries into Britain and elsewhere in Europe."

"Well, that part is true. I suppose I have seen odd pieces in the newspapers about illegal women immigrants being arrested here while involved in prostitution and other criminal activities."

Later at home, Donny studied a document Jonathon had left with them. Then he read aloud. "The British end of the chain is being handled by the security services and the CID. The main thrust of this smuggling is the sex trade. The average age of the slaves is thirteen, and includes both sexes. The most valuable are the untouched, the virgin girls. They alone command the highest prices. They are, to a large extent, re-exported to far-eastern buyers, who pay well for the condition. Of the others, the paedophile market is brisk for the younger imports of both sexes. For the older-looking girls and boys, it's prostitution. The young people are being purchased by the gangs found in most of the big cities throughout UK. The latest source of slaves has been from Poland, Lithuania and Latvia."

Donny stopped reading and looked at Abby. "Would I be stupid to think that perhaps Jonathon was inviting us to poke our noses into the UK end of this trade? I am inclined to think, from our conversations, that his worry is corruption at this end, causing a blind eye to be turned to the importation and the trade in general."

Abby thought about what Donny had suggested, and slowly nodded her head. "When you think of the comments he made about the Canvan family, and the fact that the son attends Brunel, I am inclined to agree with you. Anyway it would do no harm to nose around a little.

"What about the Polish man, Pavel? Is he still about?"

"He certainly is. I'll have words with him tomorrow and see what we can come up with. Meanwhile, watch yourself. That idiot, Anson, is liable to do something stupid. Make sure you don't get caught in a corner with him around."

The following morning Donny found the address of the Canvan family and, having, spoken in addition to one of Anson's former girlfriends, the part of the house he occupied. He had no notion of using the information. It was a question of information that may one day be useful.

Speaking to Pavel was more difficult. It was only when Pavel discovered that Abby, who was now known throughout the campus as the girl that made Anson look a fool, was actually Donny's girlfriend that he finally opened up.

He had an English girlfriend, Mary, who lived in Seer Green, just outside Uxbridge on the A40 west. It seemed that his girlfriend's twelve year old sister, Penny, was dazzled by the Orange Lamborghini, and she was foolish enough to accept an invitation to ride in it, when Anson found her looking it over in Uxbridge Market Square.

When she finally got home that night she was in tears. Her clothes were torn and she would not say anything about what had happened or how she got in the state she arrived in.

When her mother saw the state of Penny's underclothes, torn and bloody she freaked, and went to call the police. It was Mary who stopped her. At the threat of the police being called she admitted that she had gone willingly with Anson Canvan for a ride in his car. She had been flattered and he was handsome and polite. When he stopped to show her the view over the Chiltern Hills, he produced a hamper from the boot. They shared the smoked salmon sandwiches and drank the sparkling wine from the cool box. He had afterwards produced a couple of cigarettes that were made, he said, with herbal tobacco. They smoked them together and cuddled up with the seats pushed back. There was no one else around, and Anson started getting amorous, touching her through her blouse and stroking her. At that point she was quite happy enjoying the attention. However he began to get more adventurous groping and probing her under her skirt, she tried to stop him but he was too strong for her. He called her a little tease and tore her panties, and proceeded to rape her. When he had finished he drove her to Seer Green and dumped her beside the main road. He said if she reported him he would visit her mother with his friends and cripple her and anyone else in the house.

That was what had spooked Pavel. He had few friends in the area and was worried about Canvan attacking Mary and the rest of the family, despite the fact that they had not reported to the police. He was still a stranger in a strange land and felt very much on his own in the circumstances.

"He actually told me that he was trying to contact the Polish community in Ealing, but he had no idea who to talk to. After all how do you ask respectable organizations where to contact the local heavy mob?"

"I see. So where do we go from here?" Abby asked. "After all, we do at least have some idea who we are dealing with."

"True but we will have to be careful. We are very vulnerable here, especially since we have no real back-up." Donny was thoughtful. He paused for several seconds before continuing. "We still have our weapons. The trouble is we are not permitted to carry them in this country, or even have them in our possession. It does mean we have to depend on our own resources, and those of any supporters. The opposition have no such inhibitions and will be accustomed to going tooled-up. I think that's still the expression they use here."

Abby grinned. "We still have those smart Kevlar vests we acquired in USA. They will stop a knife or bullet, and they could also soften a punch. Would you like me to model mine to see if it still fits?" The mischievous smile that accompanied the offer was an invitation in itself.

The discussion from that point onward was occupied by personal matters conducted with considerable hilarity and involving a move into the more comfortable environment of the bedroom.

Chapter two

The King is dead?

Anson Canvan sat looking at the screen of the computer unbelievingly. The message was clear, no mistakes. His father was dead. The Lear-jet carrying him between two islands in the Bahamas had failed to arrive. It had dropped off the radar, one hundred miles off the coast of Bimini and it hadn't reappeared. The air-sea rescue had found wreckage and three bodies though not that of his father. His death was presumed, and in law that meant that now Anson inherited. Suddenly he was responsible for a multi-million pound organization.

The visit from the lawyer retained by his father had been enlightening to say the least. In terms of wealth, he was now a multi-millionaire. The whole transfer of funds, less taxes, would be accomplished with minimal fuss over the next few days. The will had been prepared by experts, and the pressure of influence that comes with great wealth ensured that funds were forthcoming. It was however the other side of the business that interested Anson. City-Bob Walker was the man. His name was nothing to do with London, or any other urban conurbation. The City came from the initials of Bob's earlier career as a car thief. The C T standing for car thief, to differentiate from the other villains called Bob, like Peterman Bob, known as Petey-Bob, and Bob, the pickpocket, known as Finger-Bob.

These innocent sounding names were not to be considered lightly as the owners were far from innocent. City-Bob was a formidable man with wide shoulders to go with an athletic physique. Good features and the Saville Row suits gave him an appearance that was normal, deceptively so. It fooled most of the general public he dealt with. As General Manager of the Canvan Empire he had enjoyed the confidence of his Chairman and under his control the business ran like clockwork.

Called to the residence by his new Chairman, he entered the office and sat in the visitor chair opposite Anson.

Bob did not like Anson, he had not liked his father, but he did respect him for the man of business that he was. Anson he regarded as a jumped-up, know-it-all, who actually knew nothing.

Anson ignored him for a few minutes, concentrating on a written report that he was not actually reading. He left it longer than he should have. City Bob, tired of the game, got up to leave. "Ah, Bob. Just the man I wanted to see." Anson looked up and rose to his feet holding out his hand. "Please take a seat; I would like to discuss the business with you."

Bob returned to the chair he had just vacated and waited to hear what Anson had to say.

Anson began. "How is the latest batch progressing?" He referred to the current, recently imported male and female youngsters, being groomed in the warehouse on the edge of the Slough Trading Estate.

"They are doing as well as can be expected." Bob replied warily.

"Any of them of special interest, or value?" Anson inquired casually.

"Seven virgins; the balance—sixteen girls that is—have all been used but there are no nasty diseases among them. The boys are all clean. The two HIV's have already been passed on to the Wembley mob for their Aids customers." He sat back thinking to himself, *Just what is the little shit playing at? Does he think he is just going to take over from where his old man left off?*

Anson was thinking too, and at the moment he was thinking that Bob was cruising for a bruising. His entire attitude was insolent. It was time he realized that he, Anson now ran the business. *He is allowed to make decisions, but only when I say so.* Putting his thoughts into action he said to Bob, "Who is your deputy in the operation?"

Startled at the question, Bob said, "Stubby Peters. Why?"

"Because I think you might be better employed elsewhere."

"Elsewhere? What do you mean? I was given this job by your father. He was well pleased with the way I run it!"

"Well, I am not my father. You seem to have a problem with the idea of working for me. I'll save you the bother. Perhaps this would be a good time for you to retire."

City Bob sprang to his feet furious. "Why, you cheeky little squirt. You know nothing about the business. You are not fit to polish your father's boots. You won't last five minutes without me. I'm known and respected in this business. Nobody crosses me up."

He made the mistake of reaching for the gun in his waistband.

Anson, had prepared for this moment, although his minder was waiting outside the door, he had taken the precaution of unclipping the gun kept beneath his father's desk, and cocking it before City Bob came in. It was already in his hand while Bob was reaching for his own weapon. Anson had wondered if he would be able to pull the trigger on a human being. He discovered that he could. Watching Bob's stricken look as he was thrown back by the impact of the first of three bullets, gave him more satisfaction than raping a virgin, he decided. As the door burst open and his pony-tailed minder burst in, gun in hand, the feeling of elation at his discovery caused him to laugh out loud.

Crilley shut the door, and put his gun away. Anson turned to him. "It was easy. It really was easy. Bang, bang, bang. He looks a bit less cocky now, doesn't he?"

Ben Crilley agreed with him but wisely said, "Give me the gun. I'll dispose of it. There should be a replacement in the safe." He took the gun from his elated boss, and placed it, wrapped in his handkerchief, in his inside pocket. Anson was already at the safe opening it with the combination his father had entrusted to him. Sure enough there were two guns in a drawer in the walk-in safe. Taking one, he checked it was loaded and put it in his waistband in the centre of his back. The other he tossed over to Crilley. "Under the desk, please." He watched as Crilley cocked and put the safety on the gun and slotted into the clamp under the desk kneehole.

"Send in Stubby Peters, Ben."

"Shall I get rid of that first?" He indicated the crumpled body on the floor.

"No. I think this interview would benefit from the sight of Bob's body. What do you think?"

With a wry grin Crilley nodded his agreement. "I'll fetch him in. Then he can help shift it when you're done."

***

Jonathon was cagey about the offer to look a little closer at the Canvan Organization. Although it had been in his mind to recruit Donny and Abby for that reason, with the apparent death of the old man he was not now so sure it would be sensible to recruit them. "Surely, you have quite enough to do studying for your degrees. Why would you want to get involved?"

"We happen to be already involved," Donny detailed the latest clash between Abby and Anson Canvan.

Jonathon considered for a few moments. Then, "Michael Canvan has conveniently been killed in an accident. His plane went down in the Caribbean. His body was not found but wreckage and two of his associates were. I am still not convinced. The investigations into the Continental end are continuing. As far as I know the new management has passed to your friend, Anson Canvan. The man left in charge was a guy called City Bob Walker, who has incidentally disappeared. I'm inclined to believe he is now an integral part of the foundations of the new council offices. His nominal job has been taken over by

Stubby Peters, his deputy. The underworld is waiting to see whether there will be a feeding frenzy, or a new kid on the block. If you decide to go in, go armed. I suspect my end is leaking like a sieve. I will not bring you in officially. My boss would not allow it anyway. I now seriously recommend you stay out until the dust settles."

Abby sat at the dining table in their apartment. The old blanket covering the table had the dismantled Walther PPK scattered about, each part gleaming with its thin sheen of oil. The magazine was empty. All the bullets also cleaned and lying on a soft cloth. Donny looked on amused. "Even the bullets?"

Abby said seriously, "Fingerprints have been taken from empty shells, you know. Remember, in this country there have been too many cases of convenience convictions. I would rather make sure that if I have to use this I won't need to spend time picking up shell cases, with bullets flying about. And if any are picked up by the police, there is nothing to send them directly to me." She looked at him directly and held out her hand.

Donny shrugged and removed his own gun from the waistband of his trousers. Passing it to her he said, "It is loaded and the safety is on."

Abby laid it on the blanket. "Give me a few minutes." She put on cotton gloves and started re-assembling her own gun, carefully wiping each piece before inserting it in place. When she was done, she wrapped the gun in a clean rag and set it to one side. Then she began on Donny's gun.

As she worked she said to Donny. "Where are we going to start?"

"Pavel!" Donny said. "Jonathon mentioned a lot of the girls were abducted and lured here from Poland. Let us start with him. I think he will be able to get help from one of the Polish Community centres. I noticed that there is a large community in Ealing, just a few stops down the line on the District railway."

"I'll get in touch with Pavel on Monday when we return to Uni. We probably won't see Canvan there from now on. He will be far too busy running his father's business to come and study."

"I wouldn't be too sure of that." Abby said, "There are other reasons to come to Brunel for people like him."

"Namely?" Donny's voice had a tinge of sarcasm.

"Oh drugs, loans, stolen goods. Things like that." Abby said smugly. "Oh, are you going out tonight somewhere?"

"No, why did you want to go out?"

"I wondered why you were walking around with the gun in your belt."

Donny looked startled. "Oh! Just habit I guess."

As Abby completed the cleaning of Donny's gun, he yawned and stretched, "I'm for bed, coming?"

Ten minutes later Abby snuggled down under the duvet, "I'm tired," she said. "Good night."

"Me too." Donny said.

A few minutes later Abby stirred and said "I thought you were tired?"

"I'm not that tired." Donny answered."

***

Pavel and Mary were discussing the assault on Mary's sister. "I could perhaps kill him," Pavel suggested.

Mary looked at him. "Be honest, Pavel. I know you are as upset as I am, but there is no way you would kill Anson Canvan."

"For you, Mary, I would do anything.".

She leaned forward and kissed him tenderly, "I know, Pavel, but there are limits. You cannot kill a spider because you can't bear to inflict pain. How could you bring yourself to kill someone?"

"You are probably right," Pavel admitted, "But I would like to do something about it."

Chapter three

Mugging

"It is odd, the way life sorts things out, apparently without the need for interference by anyone," Abby commented on the matter to Donny as they drove to the Campus. "Have you seen the disgustingly-colored Lamborghini lately?"

"As a matter of fact I have." Donny replied "Look over there behind the transit van, in the corner of the car park."

He nodded in the direction and swung the 2CV round to draw up, concealed by the van, out of sight of the orange car.

"Something's happening," he said to Abby. "I think it's Pavel." He left the car without closing the door, and—followed by Abby—walked around the transit van. As he suspected, Pavel was being systematically punched by two men while Anson and Crilley looked on smiling.

"Having a good time?" Donny said, kicking the nearest thug between his legs, causing him to forego his turn to punch and clutch his crushed genitals. Abby stopped her thug with a knuckle blow to the left kidney that sent her target gasping to the ground in agony.

Donny spun round in time to block the skull-crushing blow from the wrench wielded by Crilley, deflecting the weapon on downward where it actually hit Crilley's own ankle.

Abby punched Anson on the nose, causing the blood to flow. The gun that Anson was producing was lifted from his hand before he realized what was happening. Crilley was down, holding what appeared to be a broken ankle. The wrench was lying several feet away where he had abandoned it.

Donny was down beside the recumbent Pavel, who was semi-conscious. "I think we need to get this man to the hospital."

Abby looked at the others. Anson was still on his feet, holding a handkerchief to his bloody nose. "I did warn you, buster," she said quietly. "You should really watch what you are doing." She picked up the wrench with her scarf wrapped around the shaft and smashed the windscreen of the Lamborghini under his horrified gaze.

Backed up against the transit van, he banged the side with his elbow. He smirked when the rear doors opened and three men tumbled out with baseball bats in their hands.

The smile disappeared as Abby shot the first man in the foot. The others stopped abruptly.

"Drop them." The cold voice got immediate response. The three bats hit the ground despite the shout from Anson to "Do them!"

Abby turned to their employer. "Shut it, you pathetic little weasel." She turned back to the two men still on their feet. "Pick up this man," she indicated Pavel. "And carefully put him in the van." She snapped her fingers. "Keys?"

"In the ignition," One of the men said.

"I'll take the van to the hospital." She said, "You follow in the car."

Donny nodded. "What will we do with this lot? Any ideas?"

Abby grinned, as the two men closed the doors of the van. "Yes. I have an idea. Drop them!" The men looked at her in bewilderment."

"The trousers, drop them all of you, including fancy pants here." She nodded at Anson who was looking furiously around the bloody handkerchief."

The last men standing performed the operation for Crilley and the man with the shot foot.

Donny grinned, gathered the discarded trousers and disappeared behind the van. Abby climbed into the transit and started the engine. She wiped the gun where she had handled it, and as she drove off she threw it out of the window.

At the hospital, they carried Pavel into A&E between them, saying that he had been mugged and they had found him in this condition. They left their names with reception and returned to the campus in the little Citroen. The entire incident had taken less than thirty minutes. "What did you do with the trousers?" Abby asked.

"Dumped them in the litter bin at the car park in the High Street. They'll all be gone within about twenty minutes, including the change, the keys, and the wallets that were still in them." Donny said with a grin.

"How many men can you get in a Lamborghini?" Abby asked with a laugh. Abby had rung Mary from the hospital to let her know what had happened to Pavel.

When Mary arrived at the hospital, Pavel was conscious once more but in considerable pain. He was waiting for a scan to confirm the extent of his internal injuries.

Mary arrived with a stranger. A short, dark-haired man named Fredric. He was introduced to Pavel as a man from the Polish Community. He listened while Pavel told them of the ambush and beating that had followed his protest at the assault on Mary's sister. He was unable to tell them how he had made it to the hospital. Fredric, having heard the story, left as discreetly and as quietly as he had arrived.

***

In the Canvan house Anson Canvan lay in bed, propped up against a pile of pillows. His face was bandaged after the surgeon had re-aligned his nose. Abby had in fact broken it. The surgeon had made it clear that a little more pressure from the blow that had been used would have driven the bone into his brain and killed him.

Crilley knocked and limped in with a cast on his damaged ankle. Like Anson he was furious. Revenge and what he could, and would, do to their pair of assailants was uppermost in his mind. The sight of his charge lying bandaged in bed made him glad that the old man was dead. He had no illusions about what would have happened to him if he saw Anson as he was now. Michael Canvan accepted no excuses for incompetence. He shivered at the thought though his face remained immobile. "What are we going to do with them, boss?" He asked as he sat in the chair beside the bed.

"When we get hold of them, I will take great pleasure in a little personal sexual therapy with the woman. I will enjoy watching the man being used by Hatchet and Silverback. Silverback got the name in prison. He not only had a full head of silver hair, he was a very hairy man with hair all over his back, its silver colour matching the hair on his head. Both men were renowned for their shirt-lifting tendencies. Neither had a reputation for constraint or gentility. They were both cruel and depraved to everyone, regardless of sex or proclivity. Hatchet was named after his favorite tool, a fire-service axe. Used properly, he boasted, he could remove all the projecting parts of a body without actually killing the person. The gruesome pair had been partnered for years.

Anson continued. "Yes, I think I will make sure the woman watches as well. They can both learn what it means to fuck with the Canvans!"

Crilley cringed inside at the thought of what the two perverts would do to the young man. It did not occur to him that they might not actually get hold of them. It was just a matter of planning. With the right bait anything could be managed.

"Leave it for now, Crilley. Forget it, even. I have passed the matter on to the right people to arrange." He went on to talk about the selection of the next group of victims for the human auction in a week. He finished saying, "By the way, send in the blond girl from Latvia. I think she is due a lesson in how to look after her clients. She hasn't been hooked on smack, has she?"

"No, boss. She was left off the list on your instruction. When shall I send her in?"

"This evening will do. Meanwhile, make sure our two targets are watched, I do not want any more surprises!"

Crilley rose from his seat and as he left the room Anson said quietly, "No more slip-ups."

He left the room with the chill knowledge that his days were numbered. His thoughts immediately turned to how, and where should he go. How much time had he got? What could he do about the very real threat to his life, posed by the man in the room behind him?

***

Fredric Zoltan was a quiet composed individual. Most of the time, this seemingly mild man stayed well out of the limelight. His value was in his ability to be unnoticed, overlooked in a crowd and, if seen, disregarded as harmless by an observer. In truth this naturally reticent man was anything but the image he projected. The last person who ignored him in a violent situation was now dead. The last thing he saw was the knife that appeared as if by magic and disappeared equally quickly. In the interim it had done its work efficiently.

Now Fredric was discussing the situation of Pavel with colleagues in the Polish action group. The house in South Ealing was a regular meeting place for members of the club, who trained for athletic events, concentrating on contact sports, boxing, wrestling, and martial arts. They also were the protectors of the Polish community from the intrusion of criminal gangs into the area. The recent discovery of the activities of Canvan and company had now come to their attention, following the rape and assault on Penny Holmes, the sister of Pavel's girlfriend. Though she was not herself Polish, Pavel's plea for help, apparently unanswered, had been picked up. And now that Pavel had been attacked it was very much a concern, especially with the Canvan connection.

***

For Crilley it was a fraught time. With the future now so uncertain he had fewer options. Where once he had looked forward to a protected life in the bosom of the Canvan family, now it seemed that his entire world was crashing about him. The capture of Abby Marshall or Donny Weston would probably be enough to restore his position in the family. Though he was now dealing with Anson, and Anson was not his father; nor ever would be, in Crilley's estimation.

The situation with Anson came to a head on the day they captured Abby. She was in the local shopping Mall when the two men Hatchet and Silverback spotted her. Anson had now mainly recovered, though still with a plaster on his nose, the sole reminder of the damage done by Abby. He received the call in his car. "Wait and watch," he ordered, and re-directed the car to the Mall.

Parking outside the front doors of the Mall, he strode in. Crilley followed, the plaster now no longer on his ankle, the replacement bandage sufficient to keep things tight. When Anson called Hatchet he was waiting in the unused despatch room below the Mall. Abby walked in calmly, though both men had hold of her arms. She appeared to ignore them, looking quite cool and calm in the circumstances.

Anson looked at her greedily. There was no way she would get away from here. He had hoped to get both of them together. But, he shrugged, half was better than none, and he did look forward to removing that superior snooty look from that beautiful face.

The pair brought her to a halt in front of their boss. Crilley stood back. He really wanted no part of this.

Anson made his next—and final—mistake. He leaned forward, thrusting his face close to Abby's. Almost spitting he opened his mouth to speak. Abby was looking at the plaster across the bridge of his newly mended nose. She dropped the bag she was carrying still, and drew back against the restraining hands of the pair of thugs holding her. Bracing herself, she head-butted that strip of plaster on the bridge of Anson's nose. As she recoiled from the strike she flung herself up into a back somersault, wrenching her arms from the too-casual grip of her two captors, who stood there, stunned at the speed of the actions of their previously docile prisoner.

Crilley watched as Anson twitched once, gave a sigh and died. The bones from his shattered nose had been driven into his brain. The two thugs had still not reacted when Abby took advantage of the shocked state of her captors, snatched up her bag and walked out, leaving the three survivors desperately trying to decide what to do about their dead boss.

Chapter four

Resurrection.

The news reached Bimini within forty minutes. The story had first to be agreed, then edited then re-approved before being finally transmitted to the special number known only to one member of the organization.

When Michael Canvan was informed of the event he did not rage nor cry, he became cold and his face set. Despite the disappointment in the way his son had performed so far, he had hoped that he would have learned a little in his absence. Perhaps shown some signs of taking responsibility for his life. It had been a sad disappointment. It seemed he had expected too much, and now he was paying the price of his over-indulgence. It was also the time for his amazing escape to be announced, and the plans for combating the authority's attack on his labyrinthine financial arrangements to be put to test.

For two days he made careful plans. Then, by arrangement, he visited the island where a man, closely resembling his physique and general appearance had been living in the rough for the past several days.

The grey-streaked hair and stubble made his features passable at a distance. The clothing was suitably torn, and a rough bandage around the forearm covered a self-inflicted wound to give authenticity to the story to be told. Satisfied that he had done all he could to make his survival and rescue possible, he returned to Bimini and set the discovery and rescue in motion.

***

There was no hiding it. It was the story of the year. The miraculous survival of the air crash, told in the halting words of Michael Canvan.

Suitably made up to reflect the privations of the past days, his surrogate, having been filmed for the record, was now shaven and polished and back in New York, sworn to secrecy with a payment guaranteeing his silence.

Michael's performance was not questioned. Any flaw in his story was attributed to the privations of his marooning on the deserted island on the fringe of the Bahamas.

His return to the United Kingdom was announced and the interview he gave at Heathrow was carefully rehearsed before the private jet landed.

Michael Canvan did not avoid the TV or radio interviews. He had practiced his look and his manner, anticipating the time when the audience would not be quite so sympathetic. He came across as a normal intelligent, successful, businessman of middle years, even managing to deflect the questions that highlighted the ongoing investigation by the inland-revenue and the fraud squad.

For Donny and Abby, despite the sudden death of Anson Canvan, there were no apparent consequences. Certainly Abby suffered reaction to the death of Anson Canvan. As she said to Donny in the privacy of their room, "Death in such a personal conflict is not the same as in a gun battle. I know he was going to hurt me—and you—if he got hold of you. I realize that I was fighting for my life. But it doesn't alter the fact that he was up close and personal, and that I knew what I did could kill him."

The inquest into the death of Anson Canvan found that death was accidental, caused by a fall on the concrete stairway to the office at his Company Warehouse. There were several witnesses who all gave evidence to the tragic event.

When Abby returned to the self-defence class she ran at Brunel in the evenings, it took a serious effort for her to give her usual attention to the young men and women under training. She was still experiencing reaction to the incident with Anson Canvan.

It was with some pride she acknowledged the success of two of her girl trainees who had reacted against three would-be mugger/rapists. They had actually got one arrested, leading to the arrest of the other two. All three men had been shocked by the hurt inflicted by the two girls, in self-defence.

The lack of reaction from the organization was worrying, Jonathon in particular was concerned, especially after the miraculous rescue of the missing and believed killed Michael Canvan. The fact that the entire disappearance and rescue had been carefully stage-managed was quite obvious to him, especially after he had studied the film and the location of the island where Canvan had been marooned. He was sceptical about the lucky escape from the crashed aircraft, with the accompanying story of the tragic death of the pilot taken by a shark with the island in sight.

The calm period was interrupted by the appearance of three Polish men at the door of the apartment leased by the young couple,

When the entry phone rang there was silence after Abby answered. Donny shrugged, "Kids?"

The knock came a few moments later. Donny went to the door and looked through the spy hole. Pavel and two others stood there. He drew the Walther and cocked it, and only then—with the gun in his hand—did he open the door, all the time taking care to keep it between himself and the three men.

"Pavel? What can we do for you?"

"Donny, I have these two gentlemen from the Polish community visiting. They have asked to speak to you about the Canvan people. Can we come in?"

Both of the other two men looked respectable, but Donny called out to Abby anyway. "We have visitors, honey."

Using the word 'honey' was a warning to Abby. While Donny ushered the three men into the lounge, Abby slipped her Walther into the waistband of her jeans, under the sweater she was wearing.

Pavel was still carrying the marks of the beating he had taken, though they were pretty faded now. He got straight to the point of the visit. "The Polish community have been very concerned with the number of Polish girls and boys that are being brought into this country for immoral reasons. Young people from Latvia, Estonia, Rumania and Balkan countries seem to be arriving as well. My friends have spoken to some of the Polish girls and it seems they were recruited to act as models, or come for work for all sort of reasons. As soon as they are gathered to travel here, they find themselves seized. Some are raped and all their possessions taken. They have no money, or passport. Once they get here they are sent out to earn money as prostitutes. They are frightened to go to the police because they think they will be sent back to Poland. There their parents will learn what is happening and they will be shamed. Some think they will be imprisoned for illegal entry. Those who argue are beaten, and some just disappear, they believe, killed.

"My friends think that the Canvan people are involved. They wish to help these people but they are themselves worried. There are several ex-soldiers in the community who are willing, but they need a leader here that knows the rules, the law and so on. They also do not wish to be sent back to Poland."

The outpouring stopped. Pavel took a breath and turned to his companions then back to Abby and Donny. "You helped me before, so I thought of you now. Can you help us?"

Donny said, "You mentioned the Canvans being involved. How do you know this? What makes you think they are?"

Pavel turned to the older of the two men with him. "Kovak, tell Donny what you have found out."

Kovak cleared his throat and spoke for the first time. "I am employed as a plumber. I am called out for emergencies. I have been called for attention in a big house in Chiswick.

"I arrive and find it has many rooms and all have their own plumbing. So I work in three different rooms on the toilets and the sinks. While I work I see many men come and go. In one room there is a girl who is Polish. She is frightened but I talk quietly to her in Polish and she tells me of this. I asked if she knows who it is who arranges these things. She says she heard the name Canvan and remembers it because it is an odd name. She was called then and she had to go.

"Next time I am called to the house I am in different rooms, so I do not see her again. But I hear Polish language. House is a brothel, I think, so I tell my friends in the community. This is George, he is from the community in Ealing and he was a policeman in Poland but now is night security guard in Slough. He will take holiday if he can help fix the bastards."

He turned to Abby red-faced, "I am sorry lady that just slipped out."

Abby grinned, "I am not offended. I understand your frustration and I think we should be able to help. But we will need a little more time to find out more about the operation."

Donny nodded in agreement and said, "Have you a number we can call?"

Both men produced cards with cell phone numbers and—in the case of Kovak—a landline number also.

Donny sat with Abby after the three men left. "From what I've seen of the Canvan family, I think we have not started to feel the repercussions from the death of Anson. With the publicity following his return, Anson's father must have been forced to keep a low profile. That will not last forever. The longer it goes on the more likely we will be off guard. I think we have to go on the offensive as soon as possible, or disappear somewhere beyond the reach of Canvan."

"I agree. But if we go on the offensive, where do we start?" Abby asked seriously.

Donny looked at her with affection and smiled. It was typical of Abby to take that attitude. He shrugged. "If we have help from the Polish community we will have to lay down some rules. First how much we tell them. Then how far should we allow them to commit, if and when the going gets rough."

Abby looked at him directly. "Speak to Jonathon first?"

Donny picked up the phone and punched the speed dial number. "First: Jonathon!" He agreed.

The familiar voice at the other end of the phone acknowledged that it was indeed Jonathon. "What can I do for you two, this fine evening?"

"It happens to be raining here actually and we have a problem to discuss."

There was a brief silence following this remark. Then, "I'll be with you within the hour. Just coffee and biscuits please, nothing heavy."

The phone clicked off, and Donny replaced the receiver. He said "Let's eat before he arrives. He is not hungry."

Later that same evening, Jonathon sat back thoughtfully. "I was not aware that the son died in that way. You are of course absolutely correct. Michael will wish to exact retribution. Since he knows who you are, and will undoubtedly know where you live, it would be wise to get out of here and find a safe base from which to operate. That I can help with. The other is that his intentions—as far as you two are concerned—are probably personal. If I am right, his removal from the scene would lift the threat to you both. Though the organization to which he belongs would continue to operate with or without him. For them a low profile is vital. My own position in this matter is, as you are aware, linked with several European agencies working mainly on the European end of the chain. I believe sadly that there are too many leaks in the system. I, therefore, do not think you can take the chance that it will all go away if Michael Canvan has an accident."

Donny and Abby looked at each other. Abby's eyebrow rose expressively.

Jonathon continued, "I would have been happy to work on this end of the operation. My new boss unfortunately dictated otherwise. Of course, I have no control over you two, have I?" He rose to his feet, dropping a key on the table. "My aunt has left her apartment in my care while she is away for three months on a world cruise. The address is on the tag. The doorman is trustworthy. He'll expect you." He looked at them both steadily. "Look after yourselves. Don't drop your guard."

They saw him out, and watched the Lotus disappear along the avenue. "Let's pack!" Abby said.

Chapter five

Skirmishing

The apartment in Kew was in a modernized block overlooking the river. The doorman was a burley ex-marine named Phil Chance. He occupied the basement apartment and during the day was normally about, keeping an eye on the lobby. The security door could be operated from the desk or—in the absence of Phil—by using the key provided to all residents. There was a controlled garage beneath the block alongside Phil's apartment, with spaces dedicated to each of the apartments.

"I love the view over the river." Abby said watching the water as it flowed serenely past the moored boats on the far side. They settled in with practiced ease. Donny spoke to Zoltan and George, arranging to meet them in Kew Gardens at a point near the Pagoda, on Saturday. He suggested a family day out to give the visit authenticity. It was a popular venue for family visits.

Zoltan was very upbeat. He had identified several ex-service people who were willing to take part in stopping this traffic in young people, especially those from Poland itself. A Spust Grupa (release group) had been formed from men and women who had all undertaken training, to renew skills they had allowed to lapse since leaving their military service in Poland.

"I have seven people, two women and five men, all ex-army. The community is funding their living expenses so that they can be available 24/7 if needed. Having identified the warehouse in Slough, I have two, a man and a woman keeping an eye on the place. We have a fast-food van that parks locally. The owner is Polish. My people work with him. It saves him money and it makes an ideal viewpoint."

"Good thinking. But what if it comes to shooting?" Donny looked serious.

"You think it will?" Zoltan asked.

"I think it possible, sooner or later. Basically we are dealing with an international organization, which operates in Continental Europe, here, and possibly elsewhere. The European end is now under official investigation. This end is still not on the list though the police are aware of its existence. We will be operating without backup. Is that understood?"

Zoltan smiled grimly. "So we have a free hand." He held out his hand. Donny shook it.

"Keep the surveillance up. Abby and I will be visiting the warehouse Sunday evening. The van will not be open then, so we will need eyes with cell phones with the sound off. Can do?"

"Call when you are on your way." Zoltan lifted his hand and rejoined his friends, while Donny caught up with Abby at the Richmond Gate to the Gardens.

"How did it go?" She muttered.

"We are covered for tomorrow evening," Donny replied. "Game on!"

***

The warehouse was located on the outskirts of the trading estate—probably deliberately—so that the activities of the owners would not raise comment from unwanted observers.

The two visitors were dressed in black. They wore soft shoes. The warehouse, like most of that type of building, had few breaks in the walls, certainly at ground floor level. Windows were located about fifteen feet up and it was possible to see that some of the windows were used for ventilation, so were not completely closed.

The black transit van provided by Zoltan had the sign-writing covered by black magnetic panels. On the roof rack a segmented ladder was carried. Zoltan parked the van away from the building and he and his companion, a taciturn young man named Steve, unloaded the ladder and carried it round to the dark side of the warehouse, where they assembled it ready for use.

Abby and Donny arrived in their car. They left it behind the next door building. They joined the two Polish men in time to help set up the ladder beneath one of the partly open windows. With the two men standing to brace the ladder, Abby mounted to the window and peered through. After a few moments she breathed through her throat mike, "Donny, we can get in. Join me when I climb through the window."

Donny acknowledged her message. As he watched her bottom disappear he swiftly climbed the ladder and followed Abby into the building. She was already standing on a crossbeam. She had clipped a rope to a bolthole in the beam using a karabiner. The rope dangled down to the floor level below. There were no lights in this part of the warehouse, so Donny pulled down his night vision goggles, relics of an earlier encounter, and viewed the green scene below.

Abby was already descending the rope into what looked like an open-topped office. The warehouse at this end seemed to be devoted to administration, though there were sections that were roofed and thus anonymous.

He followed Abby down and joined her in the office. "Guns!" He whispered. Both drew their suppressed weapons, and together they left the office moving out into the area beyond.

The space was divided up into rooms. There was no sign or sound of occupancy, so Donny tried the nearest door. It opened under his hand. The scent of perfume became immediately apparent. In the room there was a bed, and dressing table with a stool. There were bottles and pots on the table and the bed had been turned down ready for occupation. A search of the room disclosed that it was used by a woman named Leah Rohm. Her passport was in the drawer of the bedside cabinet. She appeared to be an elegant-looking brunette whose occupation was given as fashion model. There was a private bathroom attached to the bedroom. The other rooms in the section were similar, two obviously occupied by males. The last room was furnished as a lounge.

By the time they had completed the survey of the immediate area, the sound of voices became apparent. A door into the section was opened and somebody entered. They heard a door slam while they were crouched down in the office. Abby guessed that the person was the woman, based on the direction of the slamming door. The sound of the toilet flush being used was followed by the door being slammed once more. The warehouse door opened and closed, and they were left alone once more.

Donny turned to Abby, he pointed upward. Abby thought for a moment, then nodded. Both climbed the rope which they coiled and lodged for future use behind one of the metal roof beams.

Then they both carefully made their way along the beams to the other section of the warehouse. The building was divided using insulating board sheets. Donny made a gap and peered through. The warehouse on the other side of the dividers had a ceiling. Light shafted through gaps and the odd hole in the ill-laid boards.. The pair was able to pry a section away to make a space for them to get through.

In order to see they used the several shafts of light that speared through the darkness of the roof cavity. They put up their night vision glasses. When they had both negotiated their way to the far end, the first thing Donny did was to ensure that they could retrace their path with less difficulty. He wedged the panel back to allow easy access. Their progress over the ceiling area was constrained by the need to keep off the vulnerable panels that made up the ceilings below them. Through gaps in the panels it was possible for them to see something of the activity in the rooms below. Abby beckoned Donny to look at the room she saw through one of the gaps. Below was a group of young people sitting on the floor. As he watched two men came in and collected six of the girls. They pushed them through the door in the corner of the room.

Abby had moved across to see if it were possible to see what was on the other side of the door. By using her knife she managed to shift the ceiling board sufficient to release another shaft of light. Donny joined her and they looked down through the new gap. Below the two men were making the girls strip off. Once naked they urged them into the row of showers. The last girl was a little slower than the others. The nearest man took the opportunity to grope her small breasts before releasing her into the company of the others.

Abby and Donny looked at each other, then moved over the roof joists to where they though the next room would be. With a little further manipulation they managed to obtain a view of what was the next step in the process. Six girls were getting dressed in an assortment of clothing. They were being supervised by two women who hurried them along to yet another door in what they deduced was a production line arrangement to prepare the young people for training or formal presentation to prospective customers.

By common agreement Donny and Abby split up to cover the remaining rooms below them. Donny found the reception area, and the showroom. It was here the girls were being shown how to present themselves to clients. It appeared that they may have been under the impression that they were learning to be models.

When they left the building and met up with
Zoltan and Steve, a pale faced Abby told them of
the other preparation room she had found at the
far side of the building. "It was a room with
plain walls and just one bed. A girl was on her
back with ripped clothing and a man raping her.
She could not have been more than thirteen or
fourteen at most." Abby was white faced and
really upset. "We must do something about this
as soon as possible." She said, "If the police are
not interested then we should do it ourselves."

One look at her white set face was enough
for Donny.

"I think we have seen enough to justify a
second visit with a little help from our friends."
He looked at Zoltan, and received a nod. "We
will need weapons."

Zoltan said, "We can arm ourselves. We
have pistols and some smg's. We can also bring
a coach to take the people away. My people will
look after them. "

Between the four they agreed a plan of action. Based on the ruthlessness exhibited by the
criminals involved, they agreed there would be
no hesitation in dealing with opposition from the
gang.

The following day was a working day and
the snack van was open for business as usual. It
was during the afternoon that the text came from

the watchers. A tractor-trailer had arrived from Budapest. There was activity at the warehouse.

Donny and Abby contacted Zoltan during a break in their program. "Tonight will be our first chance to make the maximum impact. Remember—black overalls, full ski masks, and gloves. No I.D in case of capture. We remove all casualties we suffer, if any!"

"Agreed. I will have the coach standing by in the estate but well out of sight." Zoltan was all business. "We have arranged a reception center for released personnel in premises owned by our Wembley community. People will be on standby, including a medical team. I have just been informed that a fifty-three seat coach has arrived at the venue and has been parked within the building. The driver has left the premises in a minicab. We are hoping to get hold of the cab driver. He is known by our snack-bar friend." Zoltan paused, "What about timing; we were set for 22.00 tonight?"

"Let's keep the same program. If anything breaks, we'll adjust as needed. See you all later. Good luck!" Donny put the phone away and turned to Abby.

She came into his arms and hugged him, "Oh, Donny. I'm worried and excited at the same time. It's been a while since we last dealt with the sort of people we face tonight. Remember—

this is Britain. It seems more personal some-how."

Donny was concerned. "Are you sure about this? That we are doing the right thing, I mean."

"Of course I am. It's just first-night nerves. That's all. When we get going, I'll be fine." She kissed him. "I'll check the weapons when we get home."

Donny looked at her. "I thought we agreed to remain armed until this business is over."

Abby seemed to wiggle and the Kevlar knife appeared in her hand as if by magic. "I am armed," she said with a smile. "It's much more convenient for carrying than the Walther."

***

The AK47 carried by Zoltan had a suppres-sor attached to the barrel. It was not as efficient as a silencer, but it did reduce the noise consid-erably. The others of the group had silenced automatics.

As they reached the vicinity Donny was re-lieved to see that the coach was still in place. They had been advised that the driver was booked to pick up the coach at 0300 tomorrow morning. But as Abby observed drily, "Plans can change, and often do!"

The ladder was installed as before and the raiders climbed in turn through the same window used by Donny and Abby on the last visit. Checking immediately below, the office was, as it was on the last occasion, empty. Three of the party descended and checked out the rooms below. They found two sleepers; a man and the model instructor were sharing her bed. Both were immobilized where they lay. Steve, who was leading the team, produced two hypodermics and both were asleep before the handcuffs were applied.

Steve led his team into the other section of the warehouse. He checked that the door was unlocked from the inside, and settled down to wait. The other four raiders were at the other end of the building. They had occupied an empty room—actually the lobby of the building—and established the location of the truck that had arrived earlier in the day. The reception room was very noisy, indicating that the place had received a large quota this time.

As the team moved in they encountered the first of the opposition. Two men appeared through the door into the lobby. For a moment nobody moved. When they realized the black-clad figures were intruders, the men dove in opposite directions, a practiced move, drawing guns at the same time. Donny, leading the team, got off two shots and caught the right hand man on the wing. The other man made it to shelter behind a desk, unhurt. Donny's victim managed to get into action from his place on the floor, his unsuppressed Makarov automatic making the first noise in the encounter. A burst of three shots from one of the AK's, equally loud, removed any threat from that direction. The automatic fell from the lifeless fingers of the defender with a clatter. The other man was in action, his first shots catching the Kevlar vest on Zoltan's man, Artem Lev, and spinning him round without actually wounding him. The AK spoke once more and the modesty panel on the front of the desk disintegrated in a shower of splinters. The cry of pain suddenly cut off, testified to the removal of that particular opponent.

The alarm now clearly given, the group split up, and made for their arranged targets. Donny and Abby went through the door of the first of the holding rooms, separating as they entered— guns up and ready. There were several young people huddled together in the corner. One pointed to the next door on the other side of the room. Donny charged straight to it, shooting the lock on the way. The kicked-open door revealed three men and a woman, all with guns that began firing as Donny hit the floor, rolling. Abby, angled from the first room, shot the legs out from the woman, who dropped to the floor with blood streaming from two bullet wounds. Her gun discarded, she sat looking at her broken limbs unbelievingly. The men were firing at Donny and he was rolling back and forth, shooting back without too much success. Abby shifted aim and shot one man twice in the centre of his body, just as she had been taught. The bullets threw the man against the wall behind him. His vest saved his life, but he collapsed stunned to the floor. His companion wavered at this new threat. Donny's next shot took him through the neck. His eye went blank. He dropped to the floor like an empty sack.

Abby's first man wearing the vest had been temporarily stunned and bruised. He lifted his gun once more. So Abby shot him in the head.

Donny rose to his feet and reloaded, Abby changed magazines and the pair moved on to the next room.

Zoltan and his two companions were in the garage section of the warehouse. There they encountered several men—all with their guns out—looking around for the origin of the gunshots. Zoltan opened fire without hesitation, taking down two of the men with his first burst. Artem Lev, an Estonian from Tallinn, had recovered from his shock after the near miss. He opened up on the opposing group, joined immediately by the third member of the raiding party. The clatter of ejected shell cases was added to the crackle of gunfire. The warehouse staff's handguns were no match for the AK47s which, at that range, were lethal. The entire warehouse party were strewn on the floor in seconds. Zoltan smiled grimly at the carnage. He checked over the bodies. The scent of cordite and the metallic smell of blood and excreta made no impression on him.

"Let's get on! Artem, check the truck. Sam!" The third man turned and faced him looking green in the face. "Next door! Take care. They will have been warned by now so they may be ready for us."

As Sam moved over to the other door, Zoltan took his place at the handle side. He reversed the taped-together magazines, clipping the fully-loaded one firmly in place and cocking his weapon. Watching to see that Sam also had changed magazines, he nodded then held up his left hand with three fingers. He folded them one, two, three. The short burst shredded the door around the lock. The kick from Sam made the door fly open. A shotgun blast greeted the attackers who were still sheltered by the door jambs on each side. As soon as the shotgun fired Zoltan stepped forward and sprayed the room with a burst from the AK. Sam from his angle did the same. When the two men stepped through the door they found a woman sprawled on the floor. Her dress was torn and she had no underwear covering her sex. She was bloody from abuse, but stirring slightly. Beside her was a big woman, built like a truck, her hard face still cruel in death. The shotgun was clutched in her hands. A man with an automatic was slumped in the corner of the room, the unfired gun in his lap. He was not dead but had little time left as far as Zoltan could see. He stooped beside the man. "Where are the others?" He asked.

The man looked at him blankly, "Others?"

"The other goods. Kids!" Zoltan prodded.

The man smiled. "Below. He pointed at the floor. "Belo....!" The last word tapered off with the man's dying breath.

At the other end of the warehouse, Steve and his party heard the gunfire and prepared to move in, but hearing sounds from the other side of the door, he motioned the others back, signalling them to spread out and cover the door. The voices approached and the door opened. The leader was talking to the two people behind him with his head turned, as he came through the door. All three people came through the door in a rush. They were into the room before they realized they had company. The man in front saw Steve and raised his gun. Steve shot him in the chest. The man dropped. The two women who had followed him threw their hands up in surrender. Steve motioned them through the inner door and sent the two men to tie them up with the others. He went through the open door into the other section of the warehouse. He could hear the noise of the others through the next wall but he went over to the corner where the carpet had been lifted and not replaced. There was a trap-door in the floor. Standing behind it so that he would be sheltered as he lifted it, he gripped the handle and lifted the heavy door back. He spoke into his throat mike. "I have found a trapdoor in the floor here. I need back-up."

Zoltan said, "With you in two minutes. I think there may be victims down there so watch who you shoot!"

"Just get here!" Steve growled. "I'm wait-ing."

Donny and Abby came in through the sec-ond door, via the shower room.

"Did I hear someone say the kids are down below here?" Abby asked.

"According to Zoltan, yes." Steve said. "Let's find out. He slid through the trapdoor and clattered noisily down the steps, closely followed by Donny and Abby. The area had obviously been developed in the past as a shelter, with a vaulted ceiling and doors off to each side. There was considerable noise coming from one of the rooms down the corridor. The three approached the door quietly and Abby nudged it open. The room was crowded with chattering and anxious looking girls and boys. The languages were mixed but most seemed to be able make out what each other was saying.

At the back of the room a woman was trying to get attention from the group.

Abby, Donny and Steve, slipped through the open door and started to ease through the chattering group. The woman was trying to establish order, with little success. So when Steve realized that she was the only staff member present, he lifted his AK and looked at Abby with a raised eyebrow?

Abby looked around once more, and then nodded. Steve pressed the trigger briefly. The short burst silenced the room instantly. Before the noise or hysteria could re-commence, she shouted, "Sit down and shut up!"

Her words were not understood by all, but the implications and the example of those who did understand got their attention. The group all sat on the floor looking fearfully at Steve's AK47.

Donny gestured to the woman from the staff.

She came forward and Abby asked, "What are you here for?"

The woman said, "I am their nursemaid. I look after the young people when they arrive here, and help them through the induction process." She spoke accented English.

"Where are you from?" Donny asked.

"Slovenia" she said in a guarded manner.

Donny studied her. She was dark haired and very pretty in an old fashioned way. Her hair was

cut in an elfin style that heightened her cheek-
bones, giving her an almost aristocratic look. Her
figure was slender but shapely, about five feet-
eight inches. She looked like, and could be, a
model.

"Why?" Abby asked.

The woman shrugged.

Abby left them to concentrate on getting the
young people out of the building. "Tell them to
follow him." She pointed to Steve. To Steve she
said, "Straight out to the bus. Get them aboard
and keep them quiet."

Steve nodded, and led the young people off
through the door.

Turning to the woman, Abby said, "With
me," and ushered her ahead out of the room.

The building was cleared of all opposition.
The wounded were carried out to the van. The 53
seat coach was full of the rescued young people
in the charge of Zoltan and three of his people.
Donny, Abby and their woman prisoner left in
the van followed by the coach. They closed the
gates and doors behind them.

Chapter six

Sheba's triumph

"My name is Sheba Bartok. My mother was an actress when the Russians ruled in Hungary. She was immediately taken from us to be the mistress of the pig that ran the area where we lived. My father disappeared. I mean my mother's husband. I do not know who my father is. The Russian was followed by others. I can only say that life was not improved when the Russians had gone. When that happened we believed everything would be good." She laughed bitterly at that. "Then the mafia appeared. The same secret police faces, just different titles. Mother grew older and I grew up. My fate was assured. I was taken to service the local Capo. I knew they would kill my mother and brothers, and I would become a prostitute anyway." She shrugged. "There were no real choices. And there was no way for me to fight them. When the traffic started to Britain, I managed to get this job. At least I could make the transition easier for the kids. I could certainly not stop the traffic. So here I am."

The four people were seated round the coffee table in the Kew apartment. Outside the river was reflecting the lights of the houses bordering it and the headlights of the cars crossing Kew Bridge.

Zoltan, Abby and Donny had been listening to Sheba's story. The empty coffee cups and the plate of biscuits stood on the table, disregarded, as she finished.

Abby looked at Zoltan. He nodded and said, "I see. So what now?"

Sheba shrugged. "That is up to you!"

Abby said, "We are not the police. We are private citizens. We have no right to hold you, nor would we want to."

Zoltan asked, "What do you think of your employers?"

Sheba's eyes blazed. "I know no-one here, but I would kill them all. They say the kids are better off in this country. They live in better conditions and their lives are better while their health and looks last. Yes, and even then they will be looked after by the State, if given the chance. The one thing they do not have is the choice. They are stolen like goods and sold as a commodity. Treated as things—chattels. As I said, I would kill them all given the chance."

Zoltan looked at her. "Your mother and brothers?"

Sheba looked puzzled for a moment. "Ah. My mother died early this year. She was comfortable, in a nursing home. My two brothers are both in America, California; playing computer games, or inventing them —safe and happy. They don't know anything of me. I know only what my mother told me before she died."

Abby said, "We have been threatened by the gang that was using you, and a friend from Poland was also threatened. We do not submit to threats, and that is why we attacked the warehouse. We are aware that this is only the beginning. Our friends from the Polish community are looking after the kids as we speak. They will either return them to their homes, or help them settle here. Do you understand?"

Sheba nodded slowly.

Abby continued, "As far as we are concerned, we will not stop harassing the gang until they are out of business. If it takes a bullet in the head, so be it. What I would like to know is whether you would care to join us in our fight? We work without police assistance. We risk being injured or killed. But we believe it is worth it." She sat back and looked at the others. "More coffee, I think." Rising, she collected the dirty cups and the coffee pot and took them through to the kitchen.

When she returned to the lounge, she looked at Donny. He nodded and she set the loaded tray on the table.

"I would like to join your group," Sheba said in a small voice. "I do not know guns, but I will help any way I can."

"Good!" Abby said briskly. "I'm glad that is settled. Let's have coffee and discuss our next move."

Chapter seven

Michael Canvan

"They came in the dark, dressed all in black with machine guns. They were quick and they shot everyone who carried a gun. Two men they beat and tied up, and Miss Rohm also. I was with the young people so I tried to keep them calm. We were taken in the bus and I was put out in London. I was frightened. I went to a friend and she let me stay there. Then today when I returned to the warehouse, Miss Rohm was angry and the men also. I do not know who the people were. When they spoke, it was English but with an accent like European. But I could not say where." She stopped and waited.

The Englishman waved her away and she left the office. Canvan looked at Leah Rohm and Henry Crossick, his lawyer. "What do you think?" He asked.

Henry Crossick rubbed his chin thoughtfully for a moment before answering. "Sounds like the truth to me. She has no reason to lie. Maybe your

European partners are not too happy with the deal they are getting?"

Leah Rohm's face was impassive. "Foreign accents? Perhaps Henry has a point, or are we talking about local competition using immigrant labour? Who do we know?"

"O'Brian, bloody Patrick O'Brian. He was keen on going into partnership with me on this deal. He dropped out when he realized that the setting up would cost more than he anticipated. Now I've arranged everything, he maybe thinks he can step in and take over from me."

"That would fit, especially if you factor in your apparent death. He could have planned this, thinking Anson would be an easy target. Your return was maybe too late for him to cancel things."

"Who do you know that might be able to help locate our raiding party?"

Leah broke in at this point. "Look, boss. The word is that there are new kids on the block. Nobody is coming up for this job. The goods have disappeared completely, either back to the EU or maybe scattered throughout the country. None of them had been tagged so we have no trace signals on them."

She referred to the recent innovation of injecting a micro location bug into the bodies of their imported goods. It allowed the new owners to keep control of their stock and increased the price at the point of sale. None of the stolen shipment had been tagged, so location through that manner was not possible.

Canvan turned to Leah, "Call in Stubby Peters. I need to do some planning. Meanwhile, get the place cleared up and ready for the next shipment. I don't want any more slip-ups."

Stubby Peters walked into the boss's office a little nervously. He had the impression that he might be blamed for the fiasco the other night. He had just thanked all his gods that he had not been there when the raid had occurred.

"Sit!" Canvan ordered when Stubby arrived. "What happened to City-Bob?"

"He and Mr Anson disagreed, I'm told. All I knew was that I was called. As I came into the office, City Bob was ready to be carried out."

Canvan looked at Stubby steadily for several seconds. Apparently satisfied, he got straight down to business. "First, have you got any ideas about who made the raid?"

"There is no hint on the grapevine boss. I only have a guess."

"Well, don't keep it to yourself. Share it with me." Canvan said testily.

Stubby stuttered a little before he eventually got his opinion out. "I reckon it might have been imported guns, used for this job only; possibly some Euro-mob doing a little poaching. By using the tunnel it would be easy to get to and from, with no bother."

"So, what about the goods? What will have happened to them?" Canvan actually was surprised. Stubby's idea could make sense.

"They were not tagged. What's to stop them selling them back to us next time?"

Canvan got up and went over to the drinks cabinet, "Whisky?" He said.

Stubby half rose. "What?"

"Do you want a whisky?" Canvan said impatiently.

"Y-Yes, boss. Thanks very much" he stuttered.

Canvan returned to the desk passing a glass to Stubby and sitting with his own drink on the desk in front of him. "So, Stubby, Number One Man; how do you like the job?"

"Still not quite used to it. Thanks, boss."

"Do you have any suggestions for the next shipment?"

Stubby felt he was being tested, and did not answer immediately. He sipped the whisky, feeling the burn right down to his stomach, then, "Tag the goods as they come through the door."

Canvan nodded, it made sense. It also proved that Stubby had actually thought about things.

Stubby continued, "Maximum security all the time the goods are in store, guns and alarms, the whole thing.

"Don't allow tampering with the goods in the warehouse. Keep it as strictly business premises. Send the goods on for grooming. Have the distribution teams here ready. As for sales: on-ship direct to clients, in their own vehicles. When they leave us, they become their responsibility. That would mean finding other premises for the direct sale collection. It would not do to have too many know where we live."

Canvan sat back astonished, this he had not expected. Stubby had always been thought of as number two, a follower not a leader. But here he was making suggestions that only a skilled planner would be expected to come up with.

Canvan rose to his feet, hastily followed by Stubby. "Finish your drink, Stubby. I will make sure that your pay is raised to cover the extra responsibilities of your new job." He put his arm round his shoulder. "See to all the arrangements, exactly as you laid them out. I want no further slip-ups. I'll sort out the new sales premises."

***

Steve had been keeping a watch on the warehouse alternating with two other volunteers. He rang Zoltan to report that there were alterations being carried out at the warehouse. A team of builders and carpenters were rearranging the layout of the building. It looked to Steve's eyes as if they were turning the premises into a drive-through arrangement with an entrance and exit through a second door at the rear of the building. A new parking area had been created at the expense of part of the accommodation in the warehouse.

The report from Sheba confirmed the information. At a face to face meeting with Zoltan, Sheba drew a plan of the new layout. She also was able to detail the new systems introduced by Michael Canvan's new manager, Stubby Peters.

Sheba had been re-assigned to the office, her duties as nursemaid being passed on to Leah Rohm. Although nothing had been said, and there was certainly no reason to suspect that she was no longer trusted, it did mean that alternative plans would be needed to ensure her safety when they closed the operation down. The ruthlessness of the operators involved in the traffic was proven. The last thing any of the team wanted was casualties.

Donny and Abby had not been involved in any repercussions from the death of Anson Canvan, yet. They had no illusions that Canvan would forgive or forget about their part in his death, whatever the official conclusions were. Both were now armed at all times, and they kept a close eye out for each other.

For Sheba, life had taken a turn that surprised her. Up until now, she had always been exploited by those around her. Her new association with Donny, Abby, Steve and Zoltan had raised doubts at the start. Now, for the first time in her life, someone other than her mother actually seemed concerned with her welfare.

Her meetings with Zoltan were set up as a method of communication. He had found her a new apartment in South Ealing. It was more appropriate for her job in Canvan's office, and within easy reach of the premises. Without the demand of regular travel to Europe, she had needed a place where she would be able to be comfortable on a more permanent basis rather than the string of temporary digs that she had been forced to use since she had moved to Britain.

After the first couple of meetings, under the guise of flat hunting, it was going to be awkward communicating with Zoltan on a regular basis. Despite his rather stiff exterior, Sheba found herself looking forward to her regular reporting sessions. Zoltan was a widower. His wife had been his boyhood sweetheart. They had married before coming to Britain but shortly after their arrival she had been diagnosed with cancer of the cervix, and despite the best efforts of the National Health she had succumbed. Zoltan's marriage had only lasted four years. Since then, he had not considered more than passing acquaintance with women.

Abby met with them both at their first arranged meeting after the apartment deal had been completed. The subject of communication came up.

"It is going to be difficult meeting after this. Now I have found somewhere to stay we have no more excuses to meet," Sheba said a little wistfully. "I suppose I could meet with you, Abby, but the Canvans know of you. It would be difficult to keep meeting Zoltan....?" She hesitated, and then continued, surprisingly a little shyly, "Unless we had a reason to meet, apart from business?"

Abby thought for a moment. Then Abby said "Of course, you get together!"

Zoltan looked puzzled?

Sheba laughed. "You mean girl and boy-friend. Zoltan fancied me, after helping me find the apartment and asks me out!" She turned to Zoltan. "Would it be such a problem?" Her laugh died. "Oh, I didn't think. Of course, you have a girlfriend already!"

Zoltan flushed and looked serious. "In fact I do not have a girlfriend, as you put it. I apologise to you both. I am out of practice at, how do you put it, chatting-up beautiful women."

To Abby's surprise, Sheba blushed in turn. "You think I am beautiful, Zoltan?"

Zoltan was red faced and looked flustered, most unlike his normal impassive self.

Abby broke in, "If I may interfere here, I suggest that, if it is agreeable, you actually start going out together, as a couple. It does mean you will need to begin to show growing affection, closeness between you. It would be necessary for Zoltan to stay overnight on occasion. The apartment has a second bedroom that can be used when needed. Your budding romance would be the perfect cover for regular meetings." She smiled brightly at them both. "You do make a handsome couple. Sheba, take Zoltan's arm and look at him adoringly!"

Sheba did exactly that, giggling, as he, blushing, submitted. He turned to look down at her and she pushed up and kissed him lightly on the lips.

He looked stunned uncertain how to react. Then he turned and pulled her up close and kissed her in a proper manner. It was Sheba's turn to blush. Confused, she looked at him warily.

Zoltan said, "If we must play the part, it is better we play it seriously. He turned to Abby. "Right?"

Abby could not help it. She laughed. "Of course, that is exactly the way you must act, if you need to act, that is." With that cryptic comment, she left them to make their own arrangements. "I'll call later in the week," she said as she went out of the door.

Left alone, Sheba and Zoltan looked at each other. "What did she mean by that?" Zoltan asked.

Sheba shrugged. "How would I know? You have lived here longer than I. If you don't know, why would I?" She looked at her watch. So I'll expect to meet you about six tonight. Will that be okay?"

Zoltan looked confused. "Tonight? Of course. But when? Where?"

"Zoltan, you fancy me. Right?"

He thought for a moment, looking quite serious and Sheba held her breath. Eventually he said "Yes, I believe I do!" His smile gave away the fact that he had been teasing her.

Relieved, she took hold of the lapels of his jacked and tugged them gently. "So you want to see me as often as possible?"

Still teasing, he said slowly, "I suppose so. Yes!"

She tugged his lapels impatiently "Meet me at six this evening at Ealing Broadway Station. Take me to the little Italian place, the restaurant in Ealing High Street, alright?"

He nodded.

"Good!" She said, reached up and kissed him lightly on the lips for the second time that day and left the office.

Zoltan sat down at his desk, and touched his lips wonderingly. He looked round the office. It was still familiar, but it suddenly felt incredibly empty with the departure of Sheba. He smiled the thought of meeting her at six that evening reminded him that he needed a haircut, and would need to get changed before he attended this rendezvous.

***

Abby met Donny for lunch before the afternoon lecture they would both be attending.

"Good meeting?" Donny asked.

"Oh, yes. Very!" Abby said with a grin.

"What does that mean?" Donny said uncertainly.

"We have arranged the perfect way for them to meet on a regular basis without suspicion." Abby said cagily.

"And how did you manage that?"

"Well. It was actually Sheba put the idea into my head." She hesitated, then hit her forehead in exasperation. "The devious little minx. She set it all up."

"What are you talking about?"

"They are going to play girl and boyfriend to cover their continuing to meet. I thought I had this great idea. I realize now that Sheba planned it all along. I think she's taken a fancy to Zoltan. From the looks of things he doesn't exactly hate the idea either."

Donny grinned, "Oh, is that all? I could have told you they fancied each other when we all met last week."

"You said nothing to me about it?"

"I thought you, of all people, would have already guessed." He smiled. "Let's get lunch. I'm starving."

Chapter eight

Highjack

The next shipment became due, and the word went out to plan the rescue group's move. There were two serious problems. One was that the process would need to be undertaken before the goods reached the warehouse and were tagged. The other was to cover how they knew the goods were coming. Suspicion might fall on Sheba and, with Canvan, could be enough to have her removed violently.

It was for this reason that Donny proposed that they put Canvan out of business permanently. It would mean that there would be a strong possibility of people being harmed. "I want it made quite clear that the traffic we are trying to stop is valuable to the people running it. They will kill to keep it running.

Zoltan and Steve were accompanied by seven other men and two women. All had served in either the police or the army. Jonathon Glynn had brought two men with him who were former SAS, both veterans of Bosnia, married to Bosnian wives who had relatives who had been stolen by the organization. The European task force were ready to strike.

Jonathon's presence was unofficial. Identifying the consignment that was under way, the truck had been allowed through. There had been no suggestion that the UK end of the organization would be closed down at the same time. For Jonathon, the embarrassment was that his masters had been slow to move, and in no way ready to legally act.

The two SAS men were introduced as Mac and Bill. Each could provide Land-Rover Defenders for the highjack. Both were reinforced vehicles from service elsewhere. The plan was to block off the tractor-trailer as it entered the trading estate. By replacing the captives with the raiding party, the vehicle would complete its journey and hopefully gain access to the warehouse. From there on everything depends on the number of people in the warehouse at the time.

Jonathon had arranged for extra weapons. Abby and Donny were left to look after Michael Canvan and whoever was present at his home/office.

It was projected that Stubby Peters would be at the warehouse with the tagging team, and the distribution arrangements. Leah Rohm would be with Michael Canvan. There were expected to be six men at the base warehouse. It was not known how many would be at Canvan's office in Corn-mill House.

***

Raphael Cortes had built an empire on other peoples misery. His base in Switzerland had been established in such a way that his privacy was assured. He also had operation sites in several other countries, mostly in the European Union. They were operated by local criminals who ran protection, prostitution, drugs and other money-making activities, all of which provided addition to his immense wealth. His particular favorite was the flesh market, as he delicately put it. He had never tired of the endless variety of female victims that passed his way. Having the selection of the cream of the beauty crop from several countries was the reason he was in the trade still. His cover was, up to now, immaculate. He was known as a philanthropist and was regularly to be seen dispensing charitable gifts to the needy when attending International charity functions.

He was surprisingly seldom photographed. The pictures that were taken always seemed to be obscured in some manner. This was deliberate because there were occasions when his substitute or sometimes one of his employees took his place. Suitably briefed, the surrogates worked well. What was not known, even by those closest to him, was that he himself was cover for another man.

It was perhaps unfortunate, an error of judgement, for him to be in Britain visiting the outlet for his favorite product at this particular time. His misfortune was that having thus far avoided any hint of stain on his spotless reputation, he managed to be in the wrong place at the wrong time, for the first time, personally.

The combination of cut-outs and deviously-routed payments had in fact insulated him from the attentions of Interpol, where neither he, nor the shadow behind him, was even considered to act in any improper way. Up until now, his personal guard force had ensured the silence of those who could have given him away.

When Donny and Abby led their party into the grounds of Cornmill House therefore, there was a prize that even Jonathon had not anticipated.

Apart from Abby and Donny, four others were present to take care of Michael Canvan and his household.

The lady ex-marine, who was Steve's girlfriend, had volunteered for this mission. Steve had asked that she go with Donny and Abby. He was worried that the raid on the warehouse would involve shooting, and he preferred she was not with him at the time. Jenna was a pretty girl, dark haired and slender. Her reflexes were whiplash sharp, and she could use a knife with finesse. The H&K smg she carried was like an extension of her arm. The three Polish lads were all ex-special forces who had stayed fit for the sheer joy of it. All had done protection service in Russia as well as Iraq. They were currently on R&R from Afghanistan. They used Glock automatics and all three had H&K smg's.

The team watched from the grounds of the house through their night-vision glasses. The lenses were adjustable and allowed them to see the laser patterns that zigzagged between the various joint boxes. The security system depended on the lasers rather than CCTV. The only cameras were mounted outside the front and rear doors, used mainly to check visitors. It was probably because of the laser system that there were no roaming security men.

The team was required to pick the way carefully between the systems of interlinking beams of light. Without the reactive glasses it would have been impossible.

Donny was surprised to discover that he had overestimated Canvan's security, and that this was the only external security. It was reassuring to find that he was wrong. The fact that they needed to move with extreme caution meant that silent concentration was used to traverse the wooded area in front of the house. The final area of lawn was partially covered by the CCTV. It was while creeping along beside the flower beds on either side of the lawn that they discovered the microphones set-up for the sound surveillance system, placed there to back up the lasers.

When the scattered group reached the front of the house itself, the plan for the entry went into action.

At the front door, in the shelter of the porch, Donny and Abby climbed the ornate Victorian stonework to the peaked roof. From there Donny was able to access the window of the second floor landing. The top of the sash window was slightly open. The age of the house meant that it had Grade 11 listing, so the windows were original. Though they were well maintained, the old wood had swollen to some extent and the window had not quite closed. The turnbuckle that should have secured the windows in place had not locked. Slipping a slender blade into the join between upper and lower windows, Donny slipped the catch clear, allowing the window to be opened. Careful to ensure that there was no electronic device. Donny slid the upper window down, the space cleared allowed him to climb through the gap created and into the upper landing of the house. Abby followed and Donny pushed the window back into the closed position, without trying to lock it.

At the rear of the house Jenna and her buddy, Hank, were poised at the door to the kitchen area. The door was not locked. There were two people in there, both visible through the window. One was a woman preparing a tray with sandwiches and a pot of coffee. The other person was a youngish man, cleaning an automatic pistol. The loaded magazine was lying on a sheet of kitchen paper, protecting the table from the sheen of oil that glinted off the metal. The man had a cloth in his hand and was wiping the exposed metal of what looked to Jenna to be a Walther PPK.

While they watched, the woman lifted the tray and said something to the man, who put the gun on the kitchen paper and rose to his feet. He opened the door for her and closed it after her.

Jenna looked at Hank. He had three fingers raised. He closed them one by one, three, two, one.

***

The Defender swung across the path of the tractor-trailer which jolted to a halt, brakes squealing. At the rear, the other Defender blocked off the trailing car. The swift deployment of the ambushers left the following vehicle stranded. The occupants were helpless under the guns trained on them.

The tractor driver jumped down and held his hands up while he was frisked and secured. The side door of the trailer was opened by the guard inside, who shouted, "What the hell is going on?" He was snatched and disarmed while the group of young people inside the vehicle were removed and loaded onto the waiting coach.

The followers from the trail vehicle were bound and gagged, and shoved inside the trailer, alongside their companions. The driver, now under guard, took his place at the wheel once more. The crews from the two Defenders parked their vehicles, climbed into the trail car and the convoy resumed its journey. No shots were fired, and no alarm was raised.

***

At Cornmill House, Donny and Abby inspected the upper floor of the house, finding no people. They did find an office used by Michael Canvan.

Having ensured that their back was clear, Donny called Jenna, "Where are you?"

"We are in the kitchen having coffee. How about you?"

"Just about to go down to the meeting in the drawing room. The upper floor is clear."

"Ready when you are."

Abby led off on her own and was in the lobby when the woman serving the coffee emerged.

"Number three, are you there?" Donny called.

The two ex-SAS men were in the security rest room. "We have two drivers here, both carrying, both now out of commission. We are ready to move on your signal."

"Roger, wait one!" Donny replied.

Abby was now at the door of the drawing room. Sitting on the floor next to her was the woman who had just been serving coffee to Canvan and his guests. Through the door she could hear the low murmur of voices.

When Donny called, Abby said nothing. She clicked the mike on and off twice, to signal that she was ready.

"Donny went quietly down the stairs to the hall below. The woman came into view, sitting on the floor beside the drawing room door. Abby, beside her, was crouched—a stethoscope poised listening to the conversation within the room. She looked up and nodded to Donny as he joined her at the door.

Donny called the SAS team. "Cover the windows of the drawing room. We will be going in three minutes."

"Roger that. Three out."

"Jenna to me. Entry in 2.5 minutes."

"Roger. Jenna out."

When the team entered, the scene that greeted them was unexpected. There were actually six people in the room. Three of them pulled guns, despite the smg's on display. Canvan, seated behind his desk, had a coffee cup in front of him and a plate with the remains of a sandwich on it. Around the room five others were seated, including Leah Rohm looking elegant, stocking-clad legs crossed. She was seated in an easy chair near the window. Her half-drawn gun never made it. Jenna fired and Leah lost interest in everything apart from the growing red stain that appeared below her right breast. The silenced Glock had made little noise.

Canvan dropped behind the desk and grabbed the gun clipped under the desk top. The three guns that were actually drawn got shots off but without result. Canvan fired and hit Donny in the side. His vest saved the bullet from wounding him, but the impact felt like a cracked rib and sent him gasping to the floor.

Abby fired three times through the top of the desk. The third shot splintered the edge of the desk. Michael Canvan, sheltered behind the woodwork, looked up and received a six inch splinter in his right eye. He reared up screaming in agony, the gun in his hand spitting bullets unaimed around the room. Without hesitation,

Abby shot him though the head. A splatter of blood painted the wall behind him as he slid down to the floor.

One shooter from the three who had actually drawn their weapons had winged Hank but he was dead already. Both the other shooters were wounded. The firing stopped.

Raphael Cortes cowered down in the settee where he had been seated. He made no attempt to arm himself and judging from the stain that spread across his groin he had been scared. One of his bodyguards was dead, the other, sat glowering at the intruders, nursing a wounded hand.

Leah Rohm was not doing too well. Her breathing was a series of gasps. Donny, back on his feet though hurting badly, gritted his teeth. "Well, Miss Rohm. This does not look too good."

"I think you have finished me." She gasped.

"Who's the visitor?" Donny nodded at Cortes.

Leah grimaced. Blood leaked from the corner of her mouth. Donny leaned in close to her.

"Bastard is the head of the snake, lives in Switzerland, cut-outs everywhere. No-one knew he was the source. He came to see his latest operation. Only Michael knew hi….mm." Her head dropped to her chest. Donny closed her eyes, and stood cautiously favouring his side.

"Collect the survivors, and their cases. Abby, call Jonathon. He should still be with Zoltan. See how they got on. We need him here to clear Michael's desk in the office, upstairs as well down here. Anyway, someone will need to clear up here."

Abby clutched Donny's hand, as they drove home after the shoot-out in Canvan's house. Donny drove one-handed most of the way. When they got in, he, sat down with Abby and held her close. "I really thought we were threatened there," he said. He winced as he twisted his sore ribs.

"Oh, Donny. I'm sorry, I was so busy feeling sorry for myself, I forgot all about your injury. Here—let's get your vest off and I'll get the arnica. You are bound to be bruised."

When she saw the bruising on his side she got to work immediately, smoothing the cream on as he lay back, wincing at even her gentle touch."

"I suppose this means I'll be off the list for tonight?" His quiet words took a moment to get through to Abby.

"Donny Weston!" She was blushing and smiling as she spoke. "You are injured. It would be very painful for you to, to…" She stuttered at a loss for words for a moment. Then, still red-faced, she said a little wistfully, "Do you really think you would be up to it?"

***

At the Slough warehouse while the raid on Canvan's house was in progress, the party led by Zoltan began with a burst of fire at the far door in the warehouse. Several shots responded, splintering the woodwork around the doorway. Zoltan jerked back, swearing as a splinter drew blood from the back of his hand. "Steve," he called.

"Here!" Steve replied. "I'm getting there. Hang on a minute." There followed two shots then the clatter of an AK47. Then Steve's voice called, "Got the bastard. You can come out now." Steve was up in the roof area, still searching for any other of the defendants toward the far end of the warehouse.

The others in the party were being led by Jonathon by the other passage, having branched off via the office beside the garage within the warehouse. Zoltan heard several single shots shortly followed by a longer burst of automatic fire then silence.

A figure appeared through the office door, making Zoltan start until he realized it was Jonathon.

Zoltan snapped, angry at himself for being jumpy. "Christ! I nearly shot him."

"All clear at this end," Zoltan said. "Three dead. Charlie got a scratch but he'll survive." As he spoke, Charlie appeared with a rag tied round his hand. He waved at the others.

Zoltan looked at his group. They had done well. "Right, let's clear the office of computer and paperwork. I want everything, mind. Load it in the truck, then load yourselves and we'll get out of here. Well done, everyone." As he turned to let them get on with it, he hesitated. "Any prisoners?" he asked.

Steve, who had rejoined the group, answered for the rest. "No survivors, boss!"

Chapter nine

The Labyrinth

Jonathon Glynn sat in the lounge of the apartment in Kew sipping Morgan's Spiced Rum and water. Sitting opposite him, his boss, Susan Mason, Deputy Director MI6, was sipping G&T and studying the report in front of her.

Donny Weston, slightly favoring his bruised ribs, and Abby Marshall were both in easy chairs drinking beer from bottles.

The room was silent while Susan Mason absorbed the report in front of her. When she finally looked up, it was Jonathon she addressed.

"What are you suggesting we do about this? As far as I can see there is no legal way we can do anything about this man and his activities." She was referring to the pattern that had emerged from the hard-drives and paperwork recovered from the Canvan episode, and Raphael Cortes in particular.

"So far," Jonathon replied. "Without any effort on our part, the ripples from the timely demise of the Canvan family have thrown up several formerly unknown pockets of interest to

Special Branch, the security services and the Serious Crime Unit, here in Britain.

"Significantly, we have also found several European sites never before suspected of illegal activity, though some have shown signs of political manipulation. The fact is that MI6 is being seriously hampered by our Euro so-called colleagues, our brothers-in-arms, who seem to think we should not be involved in what is, as far as they are concerned, an exclusively Continental concern.

"The operations that I have been involved in over the past three months have been effectively a waste of time. Matters which required instant decision were deferred for high level study. By the time action was permitted, the opposition had closed the door. Two things are indicated to me; that the organization has influence in the administration at a high level. (Information is being passed to them about everything the task force undertakes.) Add that to the lack of co-operation between us and the Americans, and we have impasse. Effectively the organization wins."

He sat back and took a swig of his rum.

Susan tapped the paper in front of her with a glint in her eye. "I repeat, what do you suggest we do about this? I do not need a list of your frustrations in dealing with Europe. I want an answer!"

Donny looked at Jonathon with a small smile on his face. It was not often that he had seen him looking uncomfortable, and at the moment he was certainly caught on the wrong foot.

Jonathon looked at his boss directly. "I have a suggestion. You may not like it, but I think I have an answer for you."

Susan sat back in the chair. "Well, don't keep it to yourself. Let us in on this suggestion I may not like."

Jonathon leaned forward composing his thoughts before he began. "During the past few years, under your predecessor, our activities on Europe were successful in assisting the authorities with the disposal of several of the most influential villains in the business.

"Our major interest was in their political manipulation of events to further their criminal aims. In the reports covering these activities there was mention of the exceptional contribution made by two anonymous, retained agents, whose identities have been protected by cover names. The names were protected to cover the fact that both were school kids. However by the time the criminals involved realized that they were in trouble, it was too late for them. The Deputy Director of MI6 was aware that their ingenuity and sheer talent were the cause of the demise of not only the leader and main movers of the gang but also of many ancillaries formerly never suspected.

"These two retained agents were targeted by successors to the original gang, who discovered that they had sealed their own fate. They tried to eliminate our agents. In the final gun battle the agents—now identified in agency terms as Mutt and Jeff—were responsible for the removal of these people, and also the Chinese involved in the attempted smear campaign on the dissident leader you may have read about at the start of last year?"

Susan Mason interrupted. "You mean that was not a French operation?"

Jonathon looked at her, now perfectly composed. "We allowed the French to take the credit, to protect our agents, and prevent them looking foolish in the eyes of the rest of the world."

"I see. So carry on."

Jonathon said, "I am done. I suggest we ask the two former retained agents Mutt and Jeff to spend some of their spare time investigating and perhaps acting in this matter, and to hell with the so-called Euro taskforce. My place in the 'force can keep them updated on whatever information we have."

His boss sat back looking thoughtful.

Abby collected the glasses and refreshed their drinks. Smiling at Donny, she gave him a beer, before seating herself once more with her own drink.

Susan stirred and looked at Jonathon. "How do we contact them? I have no information on these people."

Jonathon looked seriously at her. "If you are serious I can arrange a meeting. But I must stress, they may not be interested. If they are, then there can be no holding back of information on the basis of the need to know. From my experience and their own, having all the information could have saved the life of a friend and also saved innocent people from injury."

Susan hesitated. Then, "You are sure they can be trusted?"

At Jonathon's nod she made up her mind. "Right. I will agree."

Jonathon looked at Donny and Abby. Both nodded slightly.

"Meet Mutt and Jeff," he said to Susan. "Donald Weston and Abigail Marshall."

To say that Susan Mason was surprised would be an understatement. The carefully edited report of the events leading to the demise of the Canvan family had mentioned, but not majored on, the part played by Donny and Abby. The report of their activities in the USA was what really made the final decision certain. It secured their appointment as temporary salaried members of MI6, reporting to Jonathon Glynn as their handler.

***

The 2CV managed the long hill up into the city of Basle, leaving Saint Louis over the French border below. The ancient City spread over the hill making spectacular views over France and also along the River Rhine crossed over by the high level bridge. The pair parked the car and, cameras out, began taking pictures, just like a million other visitors.

Their actual purpose for being in Basle was to contact Marcus Weiss, a clockmaker, who had, in the past assisted MI6 on several occasions.

The premises run by Marcus Weiss were not difficult to find. The small, low-ceilinged room where he displayed his works had the atmosphere and appearance of a fairy-tale workshop from another time.

Marcus was a short, round man with a permanent smile and a generous nature. On the arrival of Donny and Abby, he immediately closed the shop and took them through to the small apartment at the rear of his premises to have coffee and cake. Frau Weiss had a more reserved manner, but she improved rapidly on acquaintance.

"Raphael Cortes is a very private person. He came to Switzerland several years ago and, with his daughter, settled in this canton without fuss. The only event to have occurred since that time was the disappearance of his daughter after an avalanche at the resort where she was on a ski holiday with friends. Seven people disappeared at that time and none have come to light since. It is believed that they were swept into a hidden crevasse on the mountain. The snow never really melts at that height.

"The search for her went on for weeks, but they found nothing except one ski which may or may not have been hers." Peter stopped at that point.

Frau Weiss said, "Sit down and drink your coffee. Peter, you should look after yourself better. What will I do without you if you drop dead from overwork before me?"

Marcus smiled. "Much better than you do now my love. I see the way Martin Voss the baker looks at you. You think I don't notice these things."

Frau Weiss blushed, smiling. "You are a silly man, Marcus. Drink your coffee."

Donny and Abby looked on, smiling at the warm raillery between husband and wife that only emphasised the profound affection between the pair.

"Where does Cortes live, Marcus?" Donny enquired casually.

"In the high country near Gempen. He has a restored Schloss there that was once the property of one of the NAZI party leaders. It was seized after the war and the place lay empty for a few years until it was bought by an old lady. She employed Raphael Cortes to re-design the gardens. When she died she left it to him."

"He doesn't sound like the master criminal we talk of today?" Abby commented.

Peter shook his head. "I have to say I have been most surprised to discover that he has become such a thing. Though he was private, he always contributed to charities and showed kindness to the people who lived on the estate. This arch-villain you describe seems so out of character."

Later that evening Abby and Donny discussed Marcus's comments. "Do you think we were talking about the same man? That creep we took at Canvan's house was a sleazy creepy type, and I, for one, was most put out when they released him because there was no evidence to hold him. The story about him being invited to discuss charitable contributions to African nations suffering from the drought was to me so much rubbish." Abby sounded disgusted.

"I agree. I think we would be justified in thinking that there could be some sort of identity confusion here." Donny mused.

"Let's pay a call on the mysterious Herr Cortes and see what happens!" The direct approach appealed to Abby. "He should not recognize us as we were masked during the entire operation at Cornmill House."

The Swiss landscape was pleasant under the late summer sun, the ever present mountains a massive backdrop to the green lower slopes. They drove through Munchenstein before turning off at Reinach, through the farmlands to locate the restored Schloss Stendhen, now the home of Raphael Cortes.

The imposing gateway to the castle grounds had both halves wide open. There was no sign of a gatekeeper, so Donny drove directly up the gravel drive to the castle half hidden in the small copse of trees at the top of a rise in the ground. As they approached, the impressive building came into view against the background of the mountains. The country beyond fell away before rising once more into the foothills about five miles away. A pattern of shades of green, grass and woods made the view quite breathtaking and it was clear why the place had been selected as the location for a castle.

The large gravel area in front of the castle was full of cars, and to one side the array of tents and stands, be-flagged and decorated, made it clear that some sort of festival or gala was occurring.

Donny parked alongside the other vehicles, and together they wandered down to the fairground.

The crowd seemed a mixture of local farmers and holidaymakers from the local area. Donny and Abby, dressed casually as they were, fitted in seamlessly as they circulated watching for any familiar faces as they strolled about.

They had been there less than a half an hour when they saw the man who had been with Cortes at Cornmill House. His hand was still bandaged from the wound he had received at the time. His was not one of the many happy faces in the crowd. In fact he looked positively sour when they first spotted him. He was watching the crowd gloomily in the company of a large man dressed in Lederhosen and white stockings. The chain round his neck with the heavy looking gold badge indicated that he was a Burgomaster at least, probably from the local town.

They watched him from then on, wandering around the fairground until the crowd began to thin out. It was then that they made their way to the castle itself.

At the door they rang the bell and were greeted by a woman dressed in a summer dress, her blonde hair styled by someone who knew what they were doing. Her eyes ignored Abby and were immediately focussed on Donny.

"Can I help you?" she asked in German. Then in accented English she said, "Pardon. How can I help you?" She smiled, though once more the smile was for Donny alone.

Abby said, "Perhaps you would let Mr Cortes know that we have called to ask him about the children's charity for East Africa. That is, if he has the time. We arrived here before we realized that it was the home of Mr Cortes, so we have had no time to arrange an appointment."

"Please come in. I will see if Mr Cortes is available. "She stood aside and indicated the door to her left which was opened sufficiently to reveal the drawing room beyond.

She closed the front door and they heard her footsteps across the hall floor, the sound disappearing as she mounted the carpet covered stairway.

A few minutes later the click of heels on the stone floor announced the return of the lady. She opened the door wide and, with a smile that looked forced to Abby's critical eye, said, "Do come through. Mr Cortes will be happy to see you in the library." She turned and led them, across the stone flagged floor to the wide staircase that divided at a landing sweeping in twin curves up to the upper level landing.

Through the central doorway they were escorted to a large pleasant room, the floor covered with an Indian rug at least 20 feet long, by15 feet wide. Settees and easy chairs were scattered about the room in a deceptively casual manner. The walls lined to the ceiling with book-filled shelves made the room feel comfortable and lived-in.

The man who stood to greet them was not the Raphael Cortes that had attended Cornmill House.

He smiled and stepped forward. "Thank you, Alicia. I'll ring if I need anything."

Their escort hesitated, obviously irritated, then turned and left the room. The man turned to the two visitors and said, "I am Raphael Cortes. What can I do for you?"

Abby spoke first. "Sir, what we have to say may take a little time, and you may find it difficult to believe, but I assure you it is true."

"Please be seated. I do apologize. I spend so much time on my own these days that I forget there are others about me." He rang a bell and Alicia appeared immediately. "Ah, Alicia. Please have tea, and pastries brought for our guests?" It was a request, but a command also Donny noted, and the response was immediate and unquestioned.

"Now, please. Who are you, and how do you come to be here?"

Donny spoke, "Our apologies, sir. We are, indicating Abby, Abigail Marshall, and indicating himself, Donald Weston, from, as you may have already gathered, England. We encountered a man who gave his name as Raphael Cortes in odd circumstances in a house in West London, in the company of what may best be described as gangsters."

There was a knock; a maid appeared bearing a tray with a silver tea service, delicate china crockery, and a serving plate with a selection of pastries.

Having laid things out on the coffee table the maid withdrew. Cortes indicated the array to Abby, and said, "Please?"

Abby poured tea for them all, and selected a pastry for herself before sitting back to listen.

"You were saying?" Cortes nodded at Donny.

"The man calling himself Cortes, it seemed, was the source of funding for the supply of young people from poor East European countries, to the international slave market. Many of the young people concerned were tricked into believing they were being recruited as models. They were then impressed into prostitution, slave labor and organ harvesting. We are both at University studying Law. We became inadvertently involved in the uncovering of the criminals involved. We decided to get away on holiday during our autumn break. Since we were here in the region of the home of Raphael Cortes, we were intrigued to discover that you were in residence despite also being in prison in England. So here we are?"

Cortes leaned back in his seat. "So what do you think now?"

Abby leaned forward and took up the question. "What I think is; either the UK villain assumed your identity to cover for himself.(Happens quite often these days,) or perhaps he was sent in the place of another. A 'Judas Goat' nominated by an enemy perhaps to implicate you, or at the least embarrass you. Of course there was always the possibility that you sent him to represent yourself, to cover-up your physical identity." She sat back and bit into her pastry.

"And what do you think, Mr Weston?"

"I think she had covered the ground pretty well." Donny volunteered.

"Do you have any idea why I should be selected?"

Oh, yes. A few; a name from the telephone book, an enemy as suggested, or a double bluff!"

Cortes sipped his tea then said slowly, "How would that work then, this double bluff?"

"A suggestion as to how I might make it work would be to send a doppelganger in my place to conduct any dealings with others. Well-briefed and well-paid of course, so that if he is caught, you hold up your hands and say, 'It isn't me, I'm here'. You, having demonstrated your distance from the whole criminal affair, would become whiter than white, not a sinner, sinned against. After laying low for a while you start the whole business up again, perhaps a different market with different products, your reputation intact."

"Proven innocent, that sounds good. In fact it is an aspect I had not taken into account." He spoke quietly, but the voice was no longer the urbane tone of their erstwhile host. It had become the menacing voice of the true character in front of them.

Abby had her Walther in her hand, concealed by her skirt. She made no move to bring it into play as yet.

Cortes continued, "I was warned that you two were a threat. At first I did not realize you were the pair that had caused the trouble in France some time ago. I had the feeling that you were a little older than you are." He laughed. "Maybe you are doppelganger, a double bluff, perhaps you are not the people you claim to be. Perhaps money might be the answer. So what do you say, £10.000, or maybe perhaps £20.000 to forget you came here? What do you think?"

Abby said, "I think that you should keep your hands away from that bell. She lifted the Walther as she spoke."

Cortes continued reaching for the bell. His hand was almost on it when Abby fired. The bullet removed the top half of the index finger and the nail section of the thumb. The suppressed gun made a phfft sound, and the blood flew. Cortes snatched his hand back savagely. Taking up the napkin from the tray, he wrapped the bleeding fingers tightly in the fabric, and looked bitterly at Abby. He said through tight lips, "You'll regret that. You are only prolonging the agony. You will never leave this place alive."

"In that case nor will you Senor Cortes," Abby said impassively. "Where is your boss? I mean your *real* boss. And where is the real Raphael Cortes.?"

The man thought about it. He studied his bloody fingers and decided to talk. "Since you will never tell anyone, I don't think it will do any harm to answer one question. Cortes is in a cell in the dungeon. You will meet him soon, I am sure. Whether he will be able to discuss his situation with you, or not, will be debateable. He smiled nastily at his thoughts on the matter. But his expression altered sharply as Abby checked with Donny. When Donny nodded, she reached forward and rang the bell.

The gun nudged Cortes in the ear as she whispered, "Just keep quiet. We will deal with the rest."

He sat stiffly, waiting, as the door opened. Alicia entered in a rush followed by a man, both carried guns.

Donny spoke from behind the door, which he quietly closed, turning the key in the lock.

"Just place them on the table gently," he ordered quietly.

The two intruders put their weapons on the polished surface of the coffee table, and stood back. "Sit down there." Abby pointed out two, deep-seated, easy chairs. When they sat in the chairs the reason for the selection became obvious. Neither would be able to leap forth from their seat to take their captors by surprise.

Donny went over to the man they knew as Cortes. "The dungeon, just where would that be?"

"Downstairs, dummy. Where else would it be."

Abby smacked him round the face with her open hand. "There is no need to be rude. You were asked a simple question, in a civil manner. I dislike people who are rude for the sake of being rude. I am beginning to think that I should shoot a few more fingers off, just to stress the point. After all, you were quite happily contemplating putting us in the dungeon with the genuine

Raphael Cortes." She turned to Donny. "What are the odds that there is a secret passage from this very room to the dungeons and elsewhere in the castle?"

Donny looked around nodded and said, "Pretty good, I would think."

"How many others are there in the castle?" Abby asked the bogus Cortes.

"You'll find out soon enough!" He sneered as he said it, then cried out with pain.

The icy voice of Donny said, "I really do not like you, and having seen the treatment your victims get and knowing about the filthy trade you are involved with, I would not lose any sleep if you started to suffer pain from broken arms and legs. I seem to recall the IRA had a habit of what they called 'Kneecapping'. That is particularly painful and permanently crippling. Now how did they do it?" He touched the right knee of the now thoroughly frightened man with the barrel of his gun. "Yes. Here I think," he stood back a little keeping his weapon in line with the man's knee.

"Three, there are only three in the castle. One is the maid who is local and works here. The others are Cortes in the dungeon and Arthur. He is keeping an eye on Cortes."

Abby went over to the curtains and removed the cords that retained them. Using the cords she tied the hands of all three. Getting them on their feet with Cortes beside her she took them down to the stone-lined area in the cellars of the castle, where, instructed by her prisoners, she located the concealed door to the hidden area of the castle foundations, on which the more modern building had been based.

Arthur, the guard heard them coming and called out. "About time, too. I'm fed up sitting here. Let me put a bullet in him and save all this nonsense."

Cortes opened his mouth to say something, so Abby slammed her gun against his head. As he collapsed unconscious to the floor, a man appeared, outlined against the light from the passage on the right. He had a drawn gun in his hand so Abby did not hesitate. She shot him twice, as she had been trained. Alicia cried out as she saw the man drop. "No, no, Arthur!" She sobbed. "You killed him! Why?"

Abby turned to her. "Because he would have killed me. Just as you would, given the chance." She picked up the Makarov automatic that Arthur had carried, and thrust it into her bag along with the other captured weapons. The passage from which Arthur had emerged had three doors, the keys for each hung on a hook beside the door. There was a light behind the first door. The others were in darkness. Abby opened the two unlit doors in turn. The light switches outside the doors worked, and each room revealed contained a bed with a mattress, a small sink and a bucket.

Though the rooms was obviously very old, the plumbing and electricity had obviously been added fairly recently.

She turned the three prisoners into the other two cells, the woman on her own, the men together. With the doors locked, Abby switched off the lights, ignoring the protests from within. Donny had opened the lit cell. Inside there was a man lying on the bed reading. "What's this?" He said as they entered, "More prisoners?"

Abby said, "Raphael Cotes, I presume?"

The man sat up. "I feel I should say, 'at your service, miss'." The voice was cultured and he sounded almost amused.

"Would you believe we have come to rescue you?" Abby said.

"From such a lovely lady I would be happy to believe anything." The man was unshaven, with receding hair. He seemed completely at ease despite the circumstances. He rose to his feet and bowed slightly. "I am in fact Raphael Cortes and this is my home. I admit I was unaware these quarters existed. I can only presume they are a relic of the refurbishment carried out by the former Nazi owner, who refrained from mentioning their presence. What purpose he had in mind when he had them upgraded is a mystery to me."

In the drawing room once more the relieved maid produced more coffee and the three were able to discuss the situation. While Abby seemed quite happy with the outcome of the visit, certain that they had now restored the true owner to his place, Donny was not quite so sure. Something about Cortes did not quite sit right. He had distrusted him as soon as he met him. He tried to mention it to Abby but she just said he was jealous because Cortes was so attentive to her. To himself, he admitted it was possible. But he was still uneasy.

Abby and Raphael went to tour the castle. Donny left them to it and fed the prisoners. Then he returned to the drawing room. He had questioned the maid about the castle. She was too young to have been around when it had been restored, but she had heard it rumored that there were secret places in the building discovered in the renovations.

Donny strolled round the bookcases at the far end of the room looking for signs of anything even slightly out of line. It was only when he examined the books in the bookshelf that he noticed the anomaly. Someone has stuck a book back in the wrong place. Automatically he pulled it out to replace it in the gap left on the shelf below. Where it had been thrust the books did not relax back to fill the gap where the book had been forced in. Curious, he tried to pull the next book out, only to discover that the so-called book was in fact made of wood, with a leather back that matched the surrounding set of real books. When he pulled the false book there was a creaking noise and the whole bookshelf began to move, pivoting on a central axis. It jammed half-open, the accumulated dust and dirt of years acting as a wedge. Donny pushed the false book back in place and the bookshelf returned to its normal position. He was excited. He was right. There were secret passages in the castle.

He looked and found a brush in the hall closet. Returning to the drawing room once more he opened the secret door. There, having swept the accumulated dust and droppings from the path of the bookcase, he watched the entrance open and close smoothly. Inside the door he found the lever which operated the system from the inside.

Determined to explore he swung the torch he carried, and identified where the passage was. It actually led off in both directions. It appeared the left hand passage would lead out to the wing of the building. Starting that way he found that there were stairs leading up to the upper floor of the building, and another flight down to the basement level. Each room he passed was acces-sible in some way, either to observe, through small movable flaps, or in the case of several rooms by both a flap and a concealed door.

Satisfied that he had seen all there was to be seen in this wing, Donny retraced his steps and took the down stairway. There he found he was behind the dungeons where the prisoners were kept. He heard their voices at first, just a murmur as he approached the voices became more distinct.

It was when he heard the name of Cortes he stopped to listen. The man who was captured with Alicia was speaking. "The boss says that we sit and wait. He'll come and let us loose. I'm looking forward to dealing with that sassy bitch. I fancy her type." He laughed, and the man who had called himself Cortes when they had arrived said, "I would enjoy a piece of that action when we get out of here."

Alicia commented, "If you two could raise your attention higher than your groin, what make you think the boss will be able to let us out? Why do you think he will want to? After all, he is as bad as you lot. He likes a bit of the other as much as you do. And we did lock him up and threaten to kill him."

The false Cortes said, "No, he cannot carry on without us. He knew we would have to let him out. The cheques require both our signatures."

"Speaking of the other, how about it, Alicia? We've got the time. What about spreading for us two to pass the time?"

"Touch me and I'll kill you, both of you bastards. Write it down and remember. I would sooner fuck the next-door neighbor's Alsatian dog than you two. Got it?"

Donny moved back to the drawing room, hearing the voices of Cortes and Abby as he closed the bookcase.

Later, with Abby alone while Cortes arranged for something to eat, he told Abby what he had heard.

Abby in turn told him, "Cortes is knowledgeable about the geography of the Castle. But considering that he has lived here for over fifteen years, he knows very little about the history of the place. And I don't like the way he keeps trying to touch me. You were right not to trust him."

"Perhaps we ought to find out what he is up to right now?" He turned to the bookcase and opened the entrance. Abby was startled, having not realized that Donny's earlier remarks had been based on hearing without being heard.

They passed through the door and when it had closed behind them Donny led her down to the dungeon observation area. The voices came through clearly. Cortes was saying. "Just shut up and wait. After the stroke you lot tried to pull you are lucky I give to the time of day. Hang on for an hour or so. I'll talk them into staying. The girl fancies me so it should be easy enough. Then I'll move when they are asleep."

"Come on, boss. What about us? I'm gagging for a bit of female attention, and I'm stuck in here."

"White they're here I cannot let you out. If it's that bad you'll just have to make do with Alicia. I'm sure she would be delighted to drop them for you." He laughed at Alicia's reaction, and left the passage to return upstairs.

Still chuckling, he walked into the drawing room, literally seconds after the bookcase was closed once more behind Donny. Abby had flung herself down in a hurry and was displaying a little more leg than she intended including a hint of her white underwear, a fact that Cortes was quick to note. Abby realized and adjusted her skirt promptly.

Cortes smiled, "You are a really attractive young lady, Abby. Donny is truly to be envied for his luck to be your friend."

"We will send the police up to the castle when we get back to town. That will save any more bother with the imposter," Donny said evenly. "We must be leaving now."

"Please stay the night. We have plenty of room. I would really like to get to know you better."

Donny held out his hand and Abby rose to her feet. "Another time perhaps, Raphael. For now we must leave. Places to go, people to see. Thank you again for your hospitality."

"Then I thank you, dear lady and gentleman, for my release and your re-assurance. You needn't bother with the police. I meant to tell you that the maid has already spoken to them."

On the way back to Basle, Donny commented, "Our friendly Mr Cortes is lying in his teeth of course."

"Of course he is." Abby smiled as she speed dialled Jonathon on her cell phone.

"Jonathon, just to let you know, Raphael Cortes is a complete phoney. I suspect the real man was removed before the accident that conveniently cost his daughter her life. Also he answers to someone else. We are not quite sure who? Whoever he is, he is powerful enough to protect them from the authorities. He is also in a position to arrange the collection and distribution of the young people. It appears the Cortes connection is more than a financial link in the chain. The Canvan family was one end. We now need the other ends. Any ideas?"

At the other end, Jonathon thought for a while. "Leave it with me and carry on and enjoy your holiday. Where are you going from there?"

"We thought we might visit Isobel and Adam. They are living in Paris. It is handy for getting about and we like Paris. If you want us we will be there."

She switched the cell off and turned to Donny. "Paris, James, and don't spare the horses."

"Very good, Milady," he said in an adenoidal voice.

"You sound just like Parker, talking to Lady Penelope in Thunderbirds." Abby giggled.

"Precisely! Any other orders, madam?" This time in his normal accent.

"I preferred Parker," Abby said still smiling.

Donny looked at her and shrugged resignedly. "Paris it is, then."

Chapter ten

The curious beggar

The building had not altered though there was a new coat of paint on the woodwork. From within, the view of the river was still the same, though the art exhibition along the railings on the riverbank had a new set of pictures.

Adam Brown had altered only as far as appearance was concerned. He looked fit and healthy. With hair trimmed and smart shirt and slacks, the camouflaged tops and cargo gear were gone and he no longer looked like an advert for an adventure magazine. Abby could see that Isobel had been a good influence on him.

Isobel Cartier had become a friend during a difficult period for Donny and Abby when they were in France last. Isobel had acquired a reputation as a dangerous lady when she had an encounter with pirates resulting in the death of her husband and daughter while sailing their own boat down the Red Sea. Believing all on board had been killed, the pirates came alongside to loot the boat. They encountered the vengeful

Isobel who was not only alive, but armed with a pump shotgun. She used it to kill all the men who boarded her boat. Then having crossed to the pirate's own boat she killed the other two. In the cabin she had found a captive family. They were earlier victims of the pirates, due to be sold in Zanzibar as slaves.

Having burned her own boat with the body of her husband on board, she offered the family the pirate's boat, an offer they refused. They sailed down to Zanzibar together, where the boat was sold. An encounter there ended with more killing of overconfident associates of the pirate crew.

The subsequent publicity made headlines despite Isobel's request for privacy. The distorted stories made Isobel more of an executioner than a victim. It did mean that on her return home to Paris, she commanded an unwanted respect among the criminal elements there. During the episode involving Donny and Abby, her reputation played a part in the outcome of the incident.

Adam kissed Abby, shook Donny by the hand and herded them into the lounge of the apartment calling for Isobel, "They're here, early as usual."

Isobel breezed in from elsewhere in the apartment looking flushed but happy to see them both. "I was just preparing your room. You took me by surprise. Wow, you do look good, Donny. Like to swap with Adam for a while? How about it, Abby?"

Abby laughed. "I'll keep it in mind. He can be a little cranky at times."

The repartee went back and forth through the preparation of food, the provision of drinks, and the sharing of memories. It was the first time they had been together since the fraught, final skirmish with the Spetsnaz two years ago. The relaxed atmosphere was enjoyed by them all. But inevitably the subject of what was happening at the moment came up.

"How are Jonathon and his lady these days?" Isobel asked.

"He is now a proud father. They live in a country house outside London, to the west, in rural Berkshire." Abby smiled as she passed this on.

Donny added, "But he is still the same old Jonathon, spook extraordinaire, currently chasing a Euro-gang exporting youngsters for immoral purposes to the UK and elsewhere."

"You are still at University in Uxbridge?" Isobel ventured.

"Yes, one more year to go. We are on vacation at the moment, just for two weeks." Abby added.

"Why would I think that you are involved somehow in Jonathon's latest project? Of course.

How else would you know?" Isobel looked at them keenly.

Donny elected to answer. "'We got involved at Uni. Jonathon was involved through Interpol and the other EU agencies. Our involvement was through a fellow student. We contacted Jonathon for help with our problem. Suddenly we became part of the big problem as the link was established between ours and theirs, as it were." He hesitated and Adam broke in,

"As it always seems where you two are concerned. Has it ever occur to you that you seem to be a magnet for trouble? You go for a cruise and finish up at war with the mob. People around you get shot. You shoot people. Your American holiday ends up with a shoot-out, and now this. What is it with you two?"

Abby smiled and shrugged. Looking at Donny she said, "Just lucky, I guess."

Donny had been sitting listening to the chat. He turned to Isobel and Adam and asked, "How long have you two been involved in this operation?"

Isobel blushed, "How did you know?"

"We haven't mentioned what happened on our American trip to anyone other than Jonathon. You must have heard it from him to know we had problems. Two plus two equals four, so you must be in touch with Jonathon. With him social does not exclude whatever concerns him at the time. How long and what has he got you doing for him?"

"Nothing really, as yet!" Isobel did not sound certain. In fact, it was obvious she was disturbed by the fact that there was a lot happening unchecked. "The main thing seems to be that nobody knows who to trust. Jonathon asked us to standby for his instructions, but that was weeks ago. We have been looking on our own and what we see is things happening, driven by bureaucrats. Official cooperation was being given to crooks."

Adam spoke at that point. "I have been watching the pattern of activity at the Government refugee centre in Bobigny. The system seems to be to gather groups of age-related people. Only every time a group is assembled they disappear. I managed to be there when a group was taken. The people who took the group away were dressed as GIGN (National Gendarmerie Intervention Group) agents, but they were not the real thing. I was able to follow them and was watching, when they took off their uniforms at a big transport depot in the western suburbs of Paris."

Isobel took over. "I contacted Jonathon's office, taking precautions of course. I passed on the information. Jonathon was not there on the number we used for contact, so I cut the contact fast. I have not heard from Jonathon since. That was over a week ago. It is most unusual for him to stay out of touch when an operation is on."

"I spoke to him two days ago." Abby said, "Using his cell number. My guess is that he has dropped out of sight because his office has leaks."

"That would explain it. We have been checking up on the Transport Depot. There seems nothing out of the ordinary. Adam had a chat with a couple of the regular drivers there, Brits. He said they see some funny things sometimes, but nothing to really put your finger on. Certainly they saw no real difference to any other of the hundreds of such places throughout Europe."

Adam observed, "The problem there is that no one wants to poke too much. If they rub someone up the wrong way, all that happens is that one day the immigration officers search your truck. Lo and behold, you have passengers. You know nothing about them, but the law says that there is no excuse. You lose your truck, your job and possibly your freedom! It makes it an easier ride for any smugglers."

Donny looked at Abby, a slow smile spreading across his face. "Shall we?" He asked.

"Why ever not!" Abby answered. "Isobel, do you still have the armory?"

"Of course. There are still far too many nasty people about to give up our independence.

What would you fancy? I have the latest H&K semi-automatic. The Glock 17 is very popular. Perhaps both?" She laughed out loud. "I am so pleased you came. It was getting a little tense being out of contact with Jonathon. It was frustrating not having the freedom to act because we were not fully briefed."

At the Immigration center at Bobigny, the scruffy, bent man made little impact on the busy life of the streets. He watched the vehicles came and going for most of the day, in and out of the attended gates of the premises. The occasional bus passed with rows of faces pressed against the windows, happy, sad, some in tears. He thought the gates should have the famous sign. "Abandon hope all who enter here,' mounted on them. Everyone entering was stopped and apparently checked, but nobody seemed concerned with the people and vehicles leaving.

The ragged man who had settled down on the pavement opposite. He had pulled a cup from his bag, and a newspaper. He sat on the paper, and put the cup beside his feet and sat, rocking gently backward and forward, humming quietly to himself.

As the day passed, vehicles came and went. The cup in front of the seated man acquired several coins. The depot closed at 17.30 and the civil servants left in an orderly stream. The quantity of coins increased sharply with the stream of homeward-bound people.

Finally, as the seated man made ready to leave, a people carrier drew up at the gate of the centre. A man in uniform stepped out and unlocked the gate. He waved the vehicle in and closed the gates behind him following the vehicle inside on foot.

The watcher noted he had not locked the gates. He turned, raised his hand to his ear and started talking. At the other end of the line the call was answered by Abby.

"Any ideas?" she asked.

Adam, the watcher, murmured, "I suspect there is a holding section normally accessed from the rear of the premises. Because they have come in the front gate, I think this may be a snatch team for a fresh supply of bodies. There is still one of the coaches parked in the yard. I expect it to exit as soon as it has been loaded with suitable stock."

Abby disliked the habit of referring to the young people involved as stock, or goods. They were, after all, people. But she contained her feelings and said, "Donny is on the way to you. He should be there in five minutes. Perhaps he will get the chance to follow and locate the next link in the chain."

Adam wandered over to the gates and, checking that no one was about, slipped through and walked over to the coach that was parked in the yard. He bent and attached a tracker to the rear bumper. Then, still not hurrying, he wandered back through the gate and returned to his place. The street was now almost deserted, most of the workers gone. Adam gathered his paper up as the black Peugeot 407 rolled to a stop and reversed into the closed factory entrance twenty meters beyond the Immigration centre entrance, on the opposite side of the road. He collected his cup, now half full, emptied the contents into a bag, and wandered off around the first corner leaving the street empty. There was no sign of movement from the Peugeot.

The rear door opened and closed quietly. Adam joined Donny, accepting the cup of hot coffee gratefully. Donny poured himself one from the flask he had brought, added sugar and sipped it, then opened the pack of sandwiches Isobel had made to sustain them for an extended wait and passed them over to Adam.

"How are things between you and Abby?" Adam asked, chewing gratefully.

"Fine thanks. Getting on OK with Isobel, are you?" Donny smiled quietly in the darkness.

"Sure, sure everything is fine between us." Adam managed to sound casual.

"What's the problem?" Donny asked. "There is obviously something bugging you."

"Well, I suppose I am getting a little restless. It's been a long time since we had any real-life excitement, and I guess I'm just a little itchy."

"I have the feeling things have just started to look up." As he spoke, he nodded at the center opposite. The gates were opening and the people carrier came through and parked over to the side of the road. The coach came next, stopping behind the people carrier, engine throbbing, while the gates were closed and locked by the same man in uniform observed earlier by Adam. He boarded the people carrier. The two vehicles moved off. "Good, the tracker is working."

Donny started the engine while Adam tuned in the tracker signal. They moved off, paralleling the course of the target vehicle from two streets away.

The chase lasted nearly one hour. There were various deviations to the route which wasted some of the time. The eventual destination was a building in Argenteuil, another fence-enclosed structure that looked like a one-time school. They approached the area and parked the car out of sight. Then on foot they were in time to see the same man closing the gates. The two vehicles were visible though the chain-link fence. Though there were some straggly bushes inside, it was possible to see the tail end of the line of people entering the building through the main door.

As they watched, Isobel and Abby joined them. They had been dropped by their taxi one street away.

"Jonathon said, 'Keep up the good work and keep in touch by cell phone'." Isobel said tersely.

"No sign of weapons, apart from the belt gun worn by the uniformed man," Donny commented.

"The youngsters probably have no idea what is going on." Abby murmured.

Isobel who had left them to walk on the other side of the road crossed and rejoined them, taking Donny's arm in a familiar manner. She leaned in and said, "There is music in the building, and other people. Is it possible that this is an innocent outing?"

The other two thought about this suggestion. Finally Donny shook his head. "Why the silent exit from Bobigny after hours? Why also all the twists and turns on the route here? They could have reached here a half hour earlier, if they had come direct!"

Abby said thoughtfully, "Perhaps they were due at a certain time?"

"Why set out so early? It would have been less trouble than an apparent random zigzag around the suburbs. The windows of the building are all barred and many are boarded up."

They had been walking around the building which occupied a block. As they reached the other side of the block they saw a fairly new signboard, next to what had been the main entrance to the building. The sign read World Charity Center. It looked new. The front door was open and there were lights and people entering and leaving. There was obviously some sort of function on, though it was not formal as the people were all casually dressed. Abby looked at Donny and Isobel in turn, "Shall we?"

"Why not." Donny and Isobel answered together.

Laughing all three joined the stream of people entering the building. They split up and joined the throng of visitors who were helping themselves to wine and canapés from the buffet tables set at the far side of what had once been the assembly hall of the original school.

There must have been over a hundred people milling about and chatting. Donny noticed three politicians, all known faces from the Strasburg Parliament. They were talking with a group of affluent-looking men and women. One lady, wearing a chain of office, was deep in conversation with a well-known face from the Brussels Euro-administration. This made the party even more of interest. Donny raised his cell to his ear and turned so that he could take photographs of the people he recognized. He then took more pic-

tures of the crowd at random. Because of the cir-
culation of the crowd he caught many more than
once. He called Abby and Isobel and suggested
they do as he was doing and use their phones to
photograph as many of the crowd as possible. It
would be of interest to Jonathon, and might help
decide what exactly was going on.

The party, they discovered, was in aid of
World Childcare. The figure of the recently released Raphael Cortes appeared from elsewhere
in the building, accompanied by the elegant
Alicia. Donny called Abby again and suggested
they leave. Isobel, who would not be recognized,
remained to keep an eye on Cortes, and perhaps
see who he spoke with.

Outside the building the pair started back to
the parked car. The attack came suddenly. The
three men erupted from the tree-shrouded entry
to one of the houses they were passing. Instinct
made Donny react, raising his hand to deflect the
club aimed at his head. The force of the blow
made it quite clear that the intention was to cause
more than minor damage. Though the blow
missed, the surprise attack nearly succeeded.
Abby stopped and elbowed the man behind her
in the face. The third man stumbled and caused
the second swing of the club to lose pace it
caught Donny in the ribs on the side opposite the
cracked rib from the encounter at Canvan's

house. He gasped and grabbed the weapon with his right hand. With the other he caught the nose of the third man and twisted it savagely, causing the man to scream in pain. At this point, Abby, who now faced her attacker, spun and high-kicked him in the throat. He dropped like a stone, gagging, trying to breathe through his battered windpipe.

Donny's opponent had released the club and drawn a handgun. As he pulled the sleeve back to cock it, he collapsed to the ground, losing the gun as he did so. The third man staggered off, holding his nose, as Adam's cheerful voice commented "I would have left you to it, but I have been too idle lately, living the easy life is bad for me."

"Where did you come from?" Donny gasped, still wincing from the blow to his ribs.

"I thought it might be a good idea to back you up. I took a little longer than I expected because I went around the other way. I just came around the corner as these guys jumped you. Where is Isobel?"

Abby said "She is still inside the reception!" She nodded towards the building across the road. They made their way back to the parked car, and were waiting chatting quietly when Isobel finally appeared twenty minutes later. The victim of Abby's boot must have been still alive. At least they were able to assume so. Certainly both of the downed men were gone when Isobel passed the location of the attack. She arrived and was given a kiss and a hug by Adam. "Thank goodness you are alright," Adam said. "I was considering coming in to rescue you."

"Rescue me? Who from? No one in there had the least idea who I was. Nor did they question my presence. It is a charity bash. I dropped some money into the bucket and got a badge for my contribution. I did not stay for the auction. Let's discuss who was there when we get back. But first, what are we going to do about the bus load of kids they brought here?"

The missile passed between the two women. Both heard it whizz past though there was no real sound from the gun that fired it. All four hit the ground and lay in the darkness, searching for any sign of the gunman. Cautiously, Donny slid his hand up the tree trunk to the point where the missile impacted. "No wonder we did not hear it he murmured. It's not a bullet. It's a bolt."

"Bolt?" Abby queried.

"From a crossbow. You know, they sell them in sporting goods shops, a sort of scaled down version of the middle ages weapon. The bolt is the size of a six inch nail, but it would kill quite easily if it hit an unprotected person."

Isobel rose to a crouch and made off to the parked car, closely followed by the others. There they opened the trunk and selected their weapons of choice. The street was quiet and the sheltered spot where they had parked was in darkness. All changed into the black overalls with hoods and ski-masks in preparation for their infiltration of the premises on the other side of the road.

Led by Adam, they set out from around the corner to prevent their being seen by the street lights which, however badly, gave some illumination to the street behind the converted school.

The fence around the school, though it concealed the area within, was not proof against the skills of the ex-SAS man, who found and opened a small gate in the fence. They passed through to the yard beyond, where they found the coach parked with the people still aboard. The driver was standing smoking, and talking with two other men beside the entry doors into the building itself.

The people in the coach were restless and there was the rising murmur of voices coming from there.

As the four intruders crouched in shadow watching, the driver broke off his conversation and boarded the coach. They heard him shouting at the passengers, telling them to be patient, and to shut up.

The noise reduced and the driver turned to rejoin his friends outside the coach. He noticed too late that the two friends had been replaced by two other people. He was secured by Donny and

Adam and placed with his friends into the luggage compartment of the coach.

Abby called Jonathon on the mobile number he had given her. He answered immediately. She explained the situation with the party in the coach, and the prisoners.

"Take them to Nanterre. There is a place, the Chateau Norde. It was used as a halfway house for the rehabilitation of wounded soldiers. It is empty except for the caretaker and his wife. By the time you arrive, my people will be there to look after things." He paused, "You seem to be making progress. Well done. Watch your backs." He rang off.

Abby turned to Adam and Isobel. "Jonathon says to take the coach to Nanterre, to the Chateau Norde. You will be met and the prisoners and passengers will be taken over and cared for."

"What about you and Donny?" Isobel asked.

"We have some unfinished business here. We'll meet back at the apartment when it is over."

She smiled, "Never a dull moment," and looked over at Donny with raised eyebrow. He nodded, went over to the closed double gates and shot the padlock apart with his suppressed automatic. Releasing the chain, he swung open the gates securing them open. There was a scurry of activity in the shadow thrown by the gate and his instinctive grab found him clutching a youngster in his mid-teens. "What are you doing here?" He said in French.

The boy swung his hand up toward Donny's face but Donny caught it before he was hit by the odd object in the boy's hand. He was clutching a hand-sized crossbow.

Donny called Abby over to help. He had his hands full holding the youngster. Abby arrived and disarmed the boy, who was carrying a quiver of bolts in a sling over his shoulder. "And that's where the bolt came from earlier. "She turned to the boy and shook his shoulder. "Why did you fire at us?"

"You stole my sister." He had an accent that was not French, though his command of French was fluent.

"We have done nothing." Abby said, "In fact we have just come here to stop the people inside."

The boy shrugged. "I thought you were some of them. I missed anyway. I'm still not used to the little bow." He nodded at the weapon now being held by Abby.

All three cleared the entrance to allow the coach driven by Adam to leave. The people carrier now stood alone in the yard. The keys were still in it and there was no sign of activity from the building as yet.

"Where are you living?" Abby asked.

The boy shrugged but said nothing.

"What do we call you?" Donny asked.

"Florien Remy!" The boy said. "We, my sister and I, came here from Guinea one month ago. We were sponsored by a charity after our parents died from fever. We were brought here in the coach and I realized that there was something not right about the business. They separated all the girls from the boys and I was able to slip away while that was happening. They took the girls off in a closed van. I don't know where."

Abby saw the glint of tears in his eyes from the street light as he finished his story.

Abby gave him the crossbow back. "Stay around while we take a look in the building. We will be back and then we will see what we can find out about your sister." She looked Florien in the eye. "We are the good guys, so wait, okay?"

The boy nodded and went to hide behind the opened gate.

"Let's go." Donny checked and cocked the Walther in his hand, then walked over to the back door of the building. It was not locked and the two stepped inside the dimly lit hallway. There was a corridor leading to a T junction and a second corridor. This was lined with the doors of what were once classrooms. There was a kitchen opposite the double doors leading into the hall. The reception was still winding down. Servers were moving in and out of the hall and kitchen, carrying trays in both directions still.

They ignored the two intruders who turned in the other direction to check out the building.

The ground floor revealed empty rooms. At the end of the corridor they came to a stairwell. Mounting the stairs without incident they found the pattern of the ground floor duplicated, though, from the sounds, they realized that some of the rooms were occupied.

There was no one in sight as they peered round the corner at the long corridor. Cautiously they made their way to the first door that had a band of light showing through the gap between the door and the floor. There was no sound coming from the room that they could detect, so Donny took a position one side of the door nodding to Abby who stationed herself on the other side. Then Danny carefully turned the handle. The door was not locked so he thrust it open and Abby swung her weapon to cover the interior.

It was an empty office, the light over the desk was on, and there were papers scattered over the desk as if someone had vacated the room in a hurry. Donny whispered, "Later?"

Abby nodded and, closing the door quietly, the couple moved down the corridor to the room where the voices could be heard.

Outside the door they listened but the speech was in a language neither could understand. The voices sounded panicky. Suddenly a French voice snapped at whoever was there. "Strip, bitch, and put on these clothes." This was followed by the sound of someone crying, then a slap of a hand on skin.

Donny looked at Abby, they both nodded. As before, they took positions either side of the door. With his fingers Donny indicated the count of three. He turned the handle slowly. Finding the door unlocked, he silently counted three, two, one, and threw the door open. Covering the room with their guns, the pair saw three girls cowering on a bed in the corner, with a big man leaning over them. There was no one else in the room. One of the girls was naked except for a pair of panties. She was crouched, covering her breasts with both arms. Her face had a red mark on the right cheek, and from the position of the man's hand he was about to hit her again. The other two girls were cowering behind their semi-nude companion, both in tears. Donny spoke quietly, his voice like ice, "Step back, slowly and carefully. Drop the dress!"

Abby, gun held steady, stepped to one side, into the man's sight line. Dropping the dress the man stepped back as instructed. Donny took the gun from the man's belt. "Turn around!" He said. When the man was facing him, Donny smacked him round the face with a full arm swing that staggered the man and startled him. The print of Donny's hand appeared on the man's face. "That's for the young lady!" Donny said. With the man's own gun he hit him hard over the head, causing the man to collapse unconscious to the floor. Abby picked up the fallen dress and flinging the dress to the girl, she ordered, "Cover yourself!"

To Abby, Donny said, "I'll take a look down the hall. Tie this guy up, then get the girls out to the people carrier. I'll follow you down when I finish here."

Abby nodded and pulling ties from her pocket she lashed the wrists and ankles of the man, adding an extra tie to join the lashings to each other, pulling the ankles up to meet the wrists. She tore the man's tie off and used it with a scrap of rag to gag him. Satisfied she indicated to the girls to follow her and led them off down the stairs. At the lower corridor there was now no activity at the far end, though noise could still be heard from the kitchen, and lights were still visible from the hall doors. They negotiated the corridor safely and made it to the vehicle outside. The four girls sat in the dark waiting for Donny to appear.

There were other rooms in use along the long corridor, and it was just bad luck that the door opposite opened as Donny opened a door on his side. The woman reacted fast. "You!" She said, and brought up the Glock automatic which she was carrying in her right hand.

Donny spun round at the sound of her voice recognizing Alicia from the Castle in Switzerland. He was going to be too late this time, though he started to lift the Walther anyway. Time stretched. He was sorry that it would end like this, though he would not have done things differently. Resigned, he suddenly became aware that a black pencil had appeared through the white blouse just below the sculpted left breast of the woman. The Glock fired but the muzzle had dropped and the bullet went somewhere else. The pencil had a blossom of red around its base and the stiffening seemed to have gone from the woman.

As she collapsed to the floor, Donny became aware of the presence of someone beside him. He turned to see Florien standing shocked at what he had done, the small crossbow hanging from his right hand.

Donny spun and turned him away from the sight of the woman's body. "Come quickly. We must get out of here. That shot will have been heard. Picking up Alicia's fallen gun, he grabbed the boy's hand and dragged him back down the corridor to the stairs.

They raced down to the ground floor. As he anticipated, people were coming from the hall end of the corridor at the run, Donny fired high twice to slow them down, and they made it to the back door without injury, despite some erratic shots from the chasing party.

As he closed the door Donny removed the key and locked it from the outside. They ran to the people carrier which was sitting, now with the engine running, waiting.

Chapter eleven

Alarms and Excursions

At the Chateau Norde near Nanterre, the coach had been parked in the stable yard by the time Donny and Abby arrived in the people carrier. The black Peugeot, which had been driven there by Isobel, was standing beside the coach.

There were several of the young people, accompanied by two adults, visible, talking and walking in the walled garden to the side of the house.

They were met by Jonathon and Marianne Glynn. The pair had met during an earlier encounter with a criminal organization in France nearly three years earlier. Donny and Abby had been involved in the encounter at the time and knew Marianne. Seeing her here was a surprise. But Jonathon explained that when he decided to use the Chateau as a refuge for the young people, he needed the place run by someone he trusted completely. So Marianne was roped in for the job.

"It seems the use of the old school building was obtained under the aegis of the World Charity Forum, an organization famous for their efforts at combining the contributions of interested charities for specific tasks." Jonathon hesitated, then thoughtfully carried on. "I have the feeling that the background of the organization needs examination. Up to now there had never been a suggestion that they were anything but clean. Some of the Directors are regarded as untouchable in the field of international charity. But of course that does not mean that they are not being used as cover."

"Where do we go from here?" Abby asked.

"Paris will be dangerous." Marianne suggested. "Perhaps you should stay here. We have plenty of room. You could help with the young people."

"Sorry, Marianne. I think I would like to get the threat out of the way before I put other people in the line of fire. If they found out I was here, they would find the kids we are looking after. Everyone would lose then. No. As long as this place is a secret it is of real value." Abby turned to Jonathon. "I presume this is a secret. You didn't get hold of it through EU sources, did you?"

"Certainly not! This has been taken for a year by Lord Carton, who anticipates buying it if it turns out to be suitable."

Donny smiled. "And who is Lord Carton, may I ask?"

"He was at school with me. He gave his name. I put up the money. It is as simple as that. We have done this before on numerous occasions."

The four were joined by Isobel and Adam at that point and they proceeded to discuss their ideas for the conduct of the next moves in the current task.

Florien had been re-united with his sister. She had been one of the three girls rescued by Donny and Abby from the old school. They had neither of them been aware at the time, it was in the people carrier when they were leaving for the Chateau that they had been re-united.

Florien had already volunteered to join the team to stop the kidnapping. Knowing his sister was now safe, and appreciating that she had been saved from a horrendous future, he was determined to do whatever he could to prevent the same fate for others.

It had been a surprise to Donny, the way Florien had so quickly recovered from his shock at the death of Alicia. The fact that it was to save Donny's life seemed to make it acceptable. Donny was not sure that Florien realized that Alice was dead, but he decided not to bring the subject up. He was toying with the idea that Florien, with his Eurasian look was at an age where he could move freely, unchecked, in Paris. There was a large population in Paris of people of colour. He would be just another youngster, where an adult might stand out. He decided to keep it in mind. It had taken a cool head to shoot Alice at the time.

Florien was fifteen years old. He had already completed his high school education before leaving Africa. It occurred to Donny that he and Abby were less than a year older when they were pitched into the events which had nearly cost them their lives. In fact they themselves had been the cause of the deaths of several individuals at that time. With a sigh, he realized that it seemed a lifetime ago that he was teaching Abby to shoot. In fact it was only just under four years.

Decision made, he turned to Abby, eyebrow raised? At her nod he said, "If you mean it, you're welcome. What about your sister?"

Florien smiled. "She has volunteered to stay with Marianne and help out here. She is a good housekeeper and she will look after the younger children with the others."

The matter settled, Donny turned to the matter at hand. Florien proudly took a place round the big table to listen. Abby said, "We really need to know where all these people live and what they are supposed to be doing." She turned to Jonathon with the question.

Jonathon produced a file from a briefcase beside his chair." I guessed we would need this.

Most of the details you mention are here. We actually ran checks on the entire staff at the children and adults refugee centres. There is little to see in them that would be of help, I'm afraid."

"Then perhaps that is where we should start," Donny suggested.

As the others looked at him with mainly puzzled expressions, Florien spoke up. "Did anyone check-out the investigators? In Africa? It would be the first place to look, I think."

Jonathon looked sharply at Florien, surprised at the interjection from the youngster. He got the point and recovered swiftly. "Absolutely! As you say, Florien, here like elsewhere, where there is doubt look for the common factor. As we know, several of these 'so-called' faultless people are in fact involved. Without them the scheme they have running could never work. We also know some of the individuals like our friend, Rafael Cortes, whoever he may really be, his man, Albert, and the fake Cortes, as yet without another name, who was at the Chateau in Switzerland."

"Losing Alicia must have been a blow. She seemed to be a major figure in the Cortes group. Replacing her will not be easy." Abby considered further. Then, "I think we find out where the next place in the chain is. We are aware of the school, and they know it. We need to keep a watch on the place to see if they shift records from the school to some other location tucked away somewhere.

Jonathon spoke, "They seem to be well organized and have been in a position to make use of whatever resources their adherents can provide. What we really need is some way of bringing the moles out of their holes. I suggest that we will never find them all. But if we can dig out the leaders, the small fry will go back out of sight and hope that they don't get found out."

"We start with those we know already, or at least suspect, and work outwards from there!" Donny's comment more or less wound up the meeting, and Jonathon, Abby and Isobel, left the two men to discussing matters.

Florien was tasked to keep an eye on the depot and take pictures of any of the visitors that he felt would be of interest. Using the phone for the purpose, the pictures could be sent to Jonathon at the Chateau for identification, where they could be fitted into a pattern, or discarded.

Adam took the job of babysitting the Raphael Cortes who had attended the Charity reception at the school. He was, according to the organizers, staying at the George V hotel. There would be little chance of the elegantly attired Adam being linked with the scruffy beggar who had appeared earlier in the area of the depot. He was provided with a souped-up Peugeot 308, in standard saloon form, parked in the hotel garage ready to leave at a moment's notice.

Donny and Abby checked into the Concorde La Fayette near Porte Maillot in Paris. It was near enough to the center of Paris to make for easy access. It was also big enough for them to drop out of sight and remain inconspicuous in the ever shifting population of tourists that used the hotel.

Isobel returned home in the meanwhile, leaving Jonathon and Marianne at the Chateau with the youngsters. They had actually been able to place most of the young people with a youth training scheme in Lille. Based on the initial teaching of the language, there was a course of training for nannies, and for the better educated girls, nursing. For the boys, graded classes to achieve further education to Baccalaureate qualifications. Run by a Religious Order, the Center enjoyed an international reputation for its dedication and results.

The last four children in the group including Florien's sister, Grace, stayed at the Chateau. Grace had been a willing volunteer to act as nanny to Jonathon and Marianne's baby. She was also keen to accompany Marianne to her home, to take up her duties. The other three were the oldest of the entire group, two girls and a boy. The boy, John Bicycle, had been rescued from his conscription into the army of one of the warlords that roamed the bush in Sierra Leone. At sixteen he was fully acquainted with the operation of most hand weapons. He had not been happy as a soldier in Africa. Having discovered the situation that he had become involved in after being rescued by Donny and Abby, he had immediately volunteered to join the team dedicated to the break-up of the kidnappers. After a demonstration of his prowess with the weapons at the Chateau, his offer was accepted. Of the two older girls who had remained, Blessed Goodbody from Liberia was his girlfriend. The other, Camille was her sister. Both girls asked to stay and help with the chores at the Chateau.

Later that day Florien departed from the Chateau and took the bus back to Paris. He was armed with his crossbow and a cell phone, both tucked into a bag. John Bicycle remained behind to act as security in the grounds armed with a Walther PPK and an over-and-under shotgun, in case—he commented—he saw a bird or two. At the sight of the gun, two Springer Spaniels living at the Chateau insisted on accompanying him, eager to join in the hunt.

In Paris the boy approached the elegantly dressed Adam with his hand out. Adam laughed at him and tossed him a screwed-up banknote and called, "Back to school with you. Boy." Florien caught the note and smiled. His attitude screamed something very rude. As he left he un-wrapped the wadded 100 euro note. Adam had passed his instructions wrapped in the note.

He took up a watch position near the school building where the Charity reception had been held. There was little sign of life there now, though all the damage done to the fence and the doors had been repaired.

Locating a space between the house wall and a builder's skip, Florien settled down to watch. Adam came onto the network to an-nounce that Cortes was on the move. Florien was startled by the vibration of the cell phone as he received the network message from Adam.

Jonathon was advised by the same process. He immediately began plotting the location of Cortes on a large scale map of the Paris area.

Florien put in the earphone he had been given and was able to follow the progress of Cortes as he moved towards the school building he was watching. He stirred from his location and stretched, preparing to get involved in a more positive way. He was nearly taken by sur-prise by the speed of the arrival of the Audi Quattro carrying the target and his two compan-ions. Albert was driving. The woman was not someone Florien knew.

Adam joined him, arriving in the Peugeot via one of the side streets where he parked the car. "There is a tracer attached to their car, so we should be able to keep them in sight even if they slip out without us seeing them. Now let's sort out how we set this job up. I will get around to the other side in case there is another car waiting. We cannot see if there is a vehicle, because of the fence around the back. If there is, I will need to know. Press the net button on your cell phone if you need me in a hurry. It will connect us immediately. I'll hear what is happening even if you cannot speak for some reason. Have you got that?"

Florien nodded.

"Good. Now if you get the chance and another car is there, this bug will stick to any clean surface. Don't take risks, but if you can get it attached, good. If by any chance you get captured press this start button and try and hide it either on yourself or drop it where it won't be seen. Now have you got all that?"

Florien grinned." I guess I'll manage. So I'll try not to get captured, yes?"

Adam grinned back at him, tapping him on the chin with his closed fist. "Yes!" He said, and swung away to find a place to keep an eye on the front of the school building.

Florien approached the back fence where the broken door had been replaced. He found a place where he was able to remove a knot in the wood and create a spy-hole.

The hand on the back of his neck was heavy so Florien did not attempt to struggle much, as the man holding him said, "What are you up to then, boy?"

Florien managed to push the transmit button on the cell phone as he said in a whining voice, "I was just looking, mister. I saw the hole and I was just trying to see what was in there. I wasn't doing any harm."

"Do I know you, boy? You look familiar. Here, you're the little bast..." The word stopped halfway as the hand relaxed and the man collapsed into Adam's arms.

"Sorry, old chap, had a little too much sauce, have we? Well, you settle down here by the fence while we get some help. There's a good chap." The cheerful voice of Adam, reassured the only passer-by who hurried by looking the other way, not wanting to be involved with apparent drunken people.

"Keep him company while I fetch the car." Adam said quietly, and disappeared. Looking about to see if he was observed, Florien checked the pockets of the unconscious man. He retrieved the 1911 Colt .45 automatic from the underarm holster and slipped it into his bag. The wallet was more difficult as the man was in effect sitting on it, it being in the hip pocket of his jeans. Florien studied it before adding it the other things in his bag. The man was called Albert

Hemmel and he came from Berne, Switzerland. This meant little to Florien, but Adam was interested when he returned.

With the trunk open, the pair taped the wrists and ankles of the man and Adam gagged him with a torn piece of towel from the trunk. They then shut Albert in, out of harm's way. Florien passed over the wallet and Adam studied the contents quickly. Then, removing the considerable amount of cash from it, put the wallet in his own bag and passed the cash to Florien. "Taxi fare and eating money, otherwise expense money. I believe Jonathon may have forgotten to issue you with any?"

"He gave me the bus fare," Florien said, "but neither of us thought about it. I have a little money of my own. I would have managed."

"I reckon you would have, but that is not the point. We can never know what is around the next corner when we are in the field. Money never goes amiss in the circumstances." When Adam spoke to Florien as if he was a fellow agent, Florien felt thrilled. He kept his voice relaxed somehow as he said, "Of course, you are right. I am learning."

Adam said, "You pick things up fast, and you stay cool. That is half the battle. I don't have any problems working with you. Now I'll get back to the front with the car this time. After all this time parking near the front entrance should not arouse suspicion."

As the car disappeared around the corner Florien returned to the spy hole in the fence and peered through. There was not too much to see. The yard was empty apart from a Toyota people carrier. The back door was closed. As he started to move away, the door opened and a man came out with a bag which he put into rear of the Toyota. He returned into the building and the door closed behind him.

Florien decided to find out what the man had put into the vehicle, so he searched for a place where he could climb the fence. At the corner he found exactly what he was looking for. Beside the road was a tree that had branches spreading over the fence. Accustomed to it at home in Guinea he climbed the tree, crawled out on the main branch and dropped to the ground. He was out of sight of the door on the other side of the fence. After waiting a few seconds to see if he had been spotted, he made his way to the parked Toyota. Opening the rear door he crawled in. The bag was on the back seat and he was able to open it from his place on the floor. He removed the file on the top of the stack and opened it. It contained lists of names grouped under headings. The names were in alphabetic order and split into male and female. The ages relating to the names were in a column alongside each name, and the groups were headed by what seemed to be a destination or origin. Certainly there were several cities mentioned, among which London and Amsterdam had the most extensive lists.

Florien was not sure what it meant but he was uneasy The London list had his name and his sister's crossed off among several others scattered between London and Amsterdam.

He returned the file, shut the case and carefully left the Toyota, closing the door to the first latch. To shut it properly would have meant slamming it, and revealing his presence.

He approached the back door and listened. There was no noise from within so he decided that the immediate vicinity was deserted. Trying the door handle he found it turned without effort, so he slipped inside.

Adam was disgusted with himself. The gun had convinced him to leave the car and accompany it's wielder across the road to the open door of the former school. Inside he had been roughly pushed into a room along the corridor running parallel to the front wall of the building. The window had been boarded up. He just managed to press the button on his cell phone before they tied him with plastic ties to a dentist's chair in what had been once the medical clinic for the school. Florien had been at the other end of the corridor when his cell phone vibrated. From what he could hear, he realized that Adam had been captured. He spotted the small group as they came through the door. There was nothing he could do at that time. But as soon as two of Adam's captors left the room, he made his way to the door and listened. He heard Adam say, "Why am I here? Who are you people? Why are you keeping me prisoner like this?" The voice sounded panicky, but Florien took no notice. He was not deceived. The other man said something from just behind the door.

Florien checked the gun in his hand, making sure there was a bullet in the chamber, then taking hold of the door handle he turned it slowly. The voice of the stranger did not falter, nor did Adam make any sound, so Florien guessed nobody had spotted the handle moving. Lifting the gun he pushed the door open and spoke quietly. "Stand still and do not make a sound!"

The startled man with the shotgun under his arm froze.

Florien eased the hammer on the gun back, the click sounded clearly in the stillness, a familiar sound to the man with the shotgun.

"Lay the gun on the floor and step to one side away from it!" Florien was cool, and sounded very serious.

The man lowered the gun to the ground and stepped aside. The door behind him swung closed and Florien walked over to Adam. "Are you alright?" Without waiting for an answer, he waved the man over. "Untie him!"

Adam said, "I don't know who you are, but, thank you anyway."

Puzzled, Florien was about to make a comment, then decided not to. Adam must have a reason for what he was saying. Florien removed the Colt from his bag and passed it to Adam. "Can you use this?" He asked.

Taking it Adam said, "I think so."

Taking the shot-gun, Florien collected the Spanish Star.38 automatic which he found in the belt of the prisoner. He tied him to the same chair with ties he found in the man's possession. The pair made their way down the corridor to the rear door. Florien described the bag he had found, and what he had seen of the contents to Adam, who decided to take the bag with them. Having disabled the Toyota, they walked out of the gate, making sure the spring lock caught when the closed it. There was no sign of the alarm being raised. The keys had still been in the ignition of the Peugeot where Adam had left them. They left the area driving sedately away, both satisfied with their night's work, ignoring the odd thump from their prisoner in the trunk.

Chapter twelve

Each day is a victory

Rafael Cortes was not amused. The reports of men missing, and more important, incriminating documents also missing, was causing him to seriously worry about the future of the organization he had helped set up so carefully. The loss of Alicia and Albert had hit him hard. They were the only people who had actually known who he was. Now both had gone and more people were becoming aware of his real identity. The use of surrogates would no longer suffice.

At the meeting in the school building it was obvious that either he did something quickly or he lost everything.

On the other side of the table sat two members of the Brussels administration. The arrangements underway were for free vehicle transit passes for parties of young people throughout Europe. No one mentioned that the parties carried were being abducted. The two officials found it convenient to be ignorant of this embarrassing information, for the sake of the money involved. On that point there was good reason for their imposed ignorance. What was really worrying Cortes at this point was finding the people to replace his two lieutenants. They had been the link between him and the foot-soldiers who actually performed the tasks, involving themselves in the hiring and firing of the various outfits which ran the prostitution and organ-harvesting in the client countries of the EU.

There were serious logistical matters to be cleared up, including the replacement of this site as soon as possible.

Arturo Massa, his former surrogate, was not as well connected or organized as Alicia. Though he had proved many times that he could be trusted, his organizational skills were sadly lacking. Before he could have used the services of the Canvan family, but they were now gone. The Paris end of the chain was not, in his opinion, to be trusted. Though on the surface they were co-operative, Alicia had always kept a close eye on all dealings with them. The two local leaders did not trust each other, and it was only by playing one off against the other that she had managed to keep them under some measure of control. Any suspicion of weakness on his behalf would be a signal to step in and take over.

This was all running through his mind as he faced the two people across the table.

The impeccably groomed woman was slender, in her forties, but still nicely shaped and attractive, until you met her eyes. Helene Blanke's eyes could change from soft and sweet to cruel and rapacious in an instant. Rumor had it that with a whip in hand she would lash a person to shreds while actually killing them, extending the agony of her victims for many hours as she satisfied her own peculiar lust. Paul Campion was of a different breed, a cruel man, in many ways as cruel as his companion, but his tastes were domination of his own sex, or small people of either sex.

Cortes despised both, and for a man of his calibre dealing in degradation and cruelty, they were in a class he would never have considered were he not desperate to get his business up and running once more.

With the financial arrangements completed, both the visitors were intent on including a sample from the supply of goods currently in transit. Cortes was not happy with the idea, but he could see no way at present of getting out of it. He promised himself he would dispose of both in the future, when things had been reorganized. Oddly, he had no doubt that the interference from the British pair Donny and Abby would be no real problem. Now he had put out official contracts on them both, he was sure their interference would cease very shortly.

***

In Montmartre—the Rue St Denis in particular—there were several places where the wise did not go. *L'Aventure* was one of these. It seemed a normal, small cafe like many others in the city. The tables were no dirtier than many others. The food was probably better than many. It was the clientele that kept the place exclusive. The Clemente brothers were the principle customers and they did in fact own half of the equity of the place. The other half belonged to Aristide Bertol, a chef of real talent. The partnership had permitted Aristide to exercise his skills. In fact the appreciation of his cooking from his partners was a major reason for the continuation of the partnership. When Chef Aristide eventually discovered the occupation which paid for his partner's share he would happily have bought them out. As things were visitors came and went, well fed and satisfied. When the brothers were present, it was a different story. Their name was Clemente and their business was murder. In their appearance there was little to distinguish them from normal members of the community, In fact from their shining shoes to their groomed hair, they were as well turned out as any other citizen of the city. They were known locally for what they were, and they carried an air of menace despite their respectable appearance. Their reputation was that they had never failed to complete a contract.

For some reason Aristide put down to that aura of menace, when the brothers were there, only fellow villains seemed comfortable in the cafe.

***

For Donny and Abby there was little time left of their stay in Paris. Whatever else needed to be done had to be done soon. They would be gone back to University, leaving things to revert to the status quo, with all the extra work that would entail.

The message came by cell phone from their agent. The twenty-first century had broken through and the criminals wore Armani suits cut to fit. They were groomed right down to the designer stubble affected by some. Direct contact was not common sense in the age of photo cameras and traceable cell phones. Contact with mechanics was always through a third party. A retained agent was the best solution for specialists like the Clemente brothers. When a contract was issued the agent would supply details through a Post Box. One of the young trainees who hung around to run messages would collect the information pack and deliver it direct to one of the brothers. They always took it from there.

At the Chateau it was the newly-recruited Florien who reported the meeting that had taken place between Cortes and two strangers, a man and a woman.

Jonathon reported that his sources had informed him that a contract had been issued for two Britons, a male and female. "From the sound of it that means you two. You will need to keep a special eye open. The word is that the Clemente brothers have been nominated."

"I take it that is not good news." Donny said drily.

"That could be the understatement of the year," was the reply.

"They are that bad?" Abby interjected.

"I'm afraid so. They are bad news in spades. It is known that they are responsible for a high proportion of mob hits here in France. I'll try to dig up a photo of them to give you some idea of who you will be facing, if you ever get the chance."

They were together at the Chateau chatting when the photo of the two visitors that had been with Cortes arrived, sent from Florien's cell phone.

Studying them Jonathon muttered, "Why would two EU civil servants from Brussels be visiting Cortes?"

"European civil servants? How do you know?" Donny queried.

"Florien sent a picture of their car. It featured an EU Commission plate. That's how."

"Ah!"

"Any ideas? Anyone?"

Eventually Marianne impatiently said," What is up with you all? The simple answer is that two people are getting paid off for some purpose. There is a lot of uncertainty in Europe these days. The scramble for position and security has always been a driving force ever since the Brussels situation was created. Despite what has always been an extremely generous financial package by any civil service standard, the continued enhancement of their pay and conditions seem to have only made them more demanding. With all the money floating about it would be naive to believe there would be no corruption in the system.

"How do we find out who these people are? After all we are 'persona non grata' in the Embassy."

"I'll show you how!" Jonathon said and picked up the phone. He spoke to someone for several minutes. The flat TV screen lit up, and a series of pictures scrolled across the surface. The scrolling stopped. The picture of the woman taken by Florien appeared one side of a split screen, on the other the scrolling resumed briefly, before stopping at a picture of the same woman. At the bottom of the screen the details of who she was and what position she occupied appeared.

The pictures shrank and moved to one side as the process was repeated with the picture of the man. When the scrolling had ceased, the two pictures were enlarged. At the foot of the display their details as transport co-ordinators brought an immediate reaction from Adam, "It will be movement warrants, certificates of authority to move from zone to zone, freely within the EU. It would guarantee that nobody would stop and search any vehicle with documents of that sort. Any attempt would require authorixation from the issuing authority. These people themselves."

He hesitated, then smiling he said, "The entire operation so far has depended on transport. Remember the comments in the truck-stop. If a driver gives trouble, immigrants are found in his truck. Innocent or not he is fined, and could lose his truck and his livelihood. So they hear nothing and see nothing, in self-defence. Whatever they suspect, or even know, about these crooked transactions, they keep to themselves. So the crooks keep operating."

He sat back and let the others mull over his comments.

Florien spoke, "What about our prisoner?"

Jonathon answered, "He is now in England, frightened out of his wits. The place he is now sitting in used to be what they call a penal servitude cell. We had it prepared for the odd occasion when we wish to impress someone. The staff employed there enjoys the chance to practice their Russian, or maybe Bulgarian, or some obscure language or other. I find it scary, and I know it's located in Epsom. We never let the prisoner know, even after release! As far as information is concerned, he was of little use. A foot soldier only I'm afraid."

"No!" The loud answer shocked them all. In the silence that followed Florien blushed and looked embarrassed. "Sorry, I didn't mean to shout. What I wanted to say is that man is not what he seems."

"Explain!" Jonathon's voice was even but there was a gritty edge to it.

Abby looked at him, surprised. It was not like him to show tension.

Hesitatingly, Florien said, "I thought I knew him when we first caught him. There was something familiar that I was not sure of at the time. I remember now where I saw him first. He was at the depot in Bobigny. He was in charge of selection, ordering the staff of the depot and the uniformed men about. The way they jumped to do whatever he said made me think he was the boss."

Jonathon gripped him by the shoulders and looked him in the eye. "You are sure it is the same man?"

Florien nodded, set faced, "I'm sure."

Jonathon snatched up his cell phone and stabbed a letter. The speed dial took a few long seconds. "Hold the X man." Jonathon sounded tense.

The reply did not please him, "Bugger!" That was as far as he would allow. He listened for a few more seconds then closed off the call.

Turning to the group he said, "We have a problem!"

Chapter thirteen

All things being equal

Nathan Arquette moved quietly through the crowd on Oxford Street in London. At a stall he bought a 'pay as you go' cell phone with a pre-paid top-up. He dialled a number as he walked, allowing it to ring three times then clicked the call off.

Five minutes later, seated in Hyde Park, the phone trembled. He picked it up and said "Yes!"

At the other end Cortes said, "Where have you been? You were on your way here. But you never arrived."

"Shut up and listen!" The phone went silent." Have I got your full attention?"

Cortes answered, his voice tight. "You have."

"I am in London. I'll explain later. Get the next shipment going to Germany, not here. The local branch here is not yet ready to handle matters."

"But why? They had a shipment two/three weeks ago. They must be ready!"

"You seem to have forgotten that Canvan's entire operation is gone. That bloody English pair, with friends, wiped them out. The last shipment and most of the earlier one have been taken away and the warehouse gutted. I have contacted a group in Acton who were customers of Canvan's, but they will need time to set up warehousing and onward shipping. As I said, send the current group to Germany. Now, what have you done about the people who took me away?"

"We did not know that you had been taken. But I have contracted the Clemente brothers to remove the embarrassment."

"Good. I was on my way in when I spotted an intruder spying through the fence at the rear. I grabbed him. The next thing I knew I woke up with a headache in the trunk of a car. I finished up in a place near London. I managed to escape, so here I am now, sitting in the park talking to you. I will contact you later, just in case this call is being monitored from your end. I will make my way to Paris and contact you again."

Arquette switched the cell off and walked over to the Serpentine . He threw the phone into the water. Turning, he strolled off along the shore line toward Kensington Gardens, On the way he sorted out the credit cards and cash taken from the two men he had killed when he escaped his captors.

Cortes put the phone down carefully. This was not good. The chief captured? He had been so careful to conceal his identity. Did they now know? What was happening now? He had done his best in the boss's absence. Had it been enough? Cortes was becoming more uneasy by the minute. Jennifer Li knocked and came in. A small half Chinese girl, she had been Alicia's choice to take over when she took on wider responsibilities. Though still not completely au-fait with everything Alice covered, she was still the best he had. She was also very pretty, a fact that he had noticed when she first joined the operation. He noted with approval the shape of the gun in the centre of the waistband of her skirt when the blouse tightened as she bent over to lay papers on his desk. He approved. There was something very erotic about the sight of the sexy body and the weapon that caused his body to react. He stretched raising his arms above his head and sighed.

"Are you okay, boss?" Jennifer asked, sounding a little concerned.

"A little tired and creaky, I guess. It has been a tense period, this last few days."

"Would you like me to give you a massage perhaps?"

With a small smile Cortes thought, *why not?* "That sounds like a great idea, Jennifer. How thoughtful of you."

***

The four friends were seated around Isobel's lounge discussing their next move when Adam brought the subject up. "The Clemente brothers are no joke. Their reputation is earned. We are not talking about bang-bang you're dead villains here. These guys are professionals, the real deal. You are probably in greater danger at this moment than you have ever been. In my opinion we should take this very seriously. Either remove the threat or talk them out of carrying it out."

"What would you suggest we do, sir?" Donny smiled to take the edge off his remark.

"Might be worth trying the talk." Adam said thoughtfully.

Abby looked at him in astonishment. "How would you suggest we do that then, mister?"

Adam grinned. "Well, we could visit their favorite haunt, sit round a table and see if there was a way we could resolve matters."

"Enough, stop it Adam!" Turning to the young couple she said. "Adam does know where they hang out. He also knows that they will not soil their own doorstep. If they are there it would be possible to talk with them, though what good it will do I cannot say. If you wish I will introduce you. At least they know me, so they won't shoot on sight." Her smile as she said this reassured them that the reference to shooting was a light hearted comment.

"What have we got to lose?" Donny said.

"They will get a chance to see us in person!" Abby said.

"And we will get a chance to see them in person." Donny responded.

"True." Abby nodded thoughtfully. "Swings and roundabouts." She added, "Let's do it. Where is this place?"

***

L'Aventure was quiet when the four friends entered. They took a table where they could see the doors to the kitchen, toilets and the street. The patron came out and, seeing Isobel, took her hand and gallantly kissed it. "Madam Cartier, welcome as always, and beautiful as ever."

"Aristide, you are still the wicked flirt I knew and loved. So do the Clemente's still come here?"

Aristide's face changed and he looked wary immediately. "They are not the sort of men you should be mixing with."

"Answer the question, Aristide. Do they still use this place regularly? And when should we expect them?"

"They still come and they will be here in twenty-one minutes."

"They are that prompt?"

"They are!"

"By the way meet my friends, Donny Weston, Abby Marshall and this is my special friend, Adam Brown. Team meet Aristide Bertol, Chef extraordinaire."

"I hope you know what you are doing," Aristide said anxiously. "The Clemente brothers look respectable, and their manners are beyond reproach, here, in public. But elsewhere?" The expressive shrug of the shoulders said it all.

"I will fetch the coffee. Perhaps you will reconsider?" He did not really believe they would. But still he departed, calling to his waitress, "Berthold, to fetch coffee for the customers."

Isobel explained that the restaurant was jointly owned by Aristide and the Clemente brothers.

Donny knew it was the Clemente brothers the moment they walked in. Had he not been expecting them at the time, the stillness that came over the place as they walked through the door would have immediately warned him of their presence.

The description fitted; the smart Armani two-piece suits, crisp white shirts with neatly knotted tie, the black slip-on shoes, highly polished, finished a picture that itself was eye-catching. The men themselves, tanned, fit looking with clean-shaven, lean faces, obviously close relatives. Of similar height and build, they carried themselves with that casual attitude of awareness that warned those around that interference could have consequences.

As they entered they assessed the entire clientele in the cafe. The first man's eyes took in Isobel and the party with her, assessing and filing the information before the smile that spread across his face and he led his brother across to greet Isobel.

There was no hesitation on either side as she allowed him to take her hands. They touched cheeks in friendly greeting. His voice was pleasant and he sounded genuinely pleased to see her. "Isobel, it has been much too long!" His brother agreed.

"Hullo, George, Eric. You are both looking well." At arm's length she looked at them both "My, you do scrub up well. The last time I saw you I was helping hose the shit off your boots after a chase through the sewers."

Eric, the other brother, laughed. "I remember. You were involved with that Chinese crook. We had just been sorting a little problem for a client. Whatever happened to that man?"

George turned and looked at him. Eric went red, "Sorry, Isobel. None of my business!"

"No harm done. In fact my friends here were involved with that little business. Do join us. I will introduce you. George and Eric Clemente, meet Abby Marshall, Donny Weston and Adam Brown."

The coffee arrived at that moment. The tension at the announcement of the names was dispersed as the waitress, Berthold, set the coffee pots and crockery on the table.

Pastries were produced and the atmosphere around the table was convivial. The cafe buzzed with the conversation of the increasing number of customers.

For Donny the situation was surreal. He sat there while the conversation flowed around him, watching and listening. There was no suggestion of any animosity or threat as far as he could see, or feel, for that matter. For all that, he could not shrug off the feeling of menace that was in the atmosphere of the cafe. He could fully understand why the cafe gradually emptied, leaving their table the sole occupants.

Isobel looked around, "Still popular, I see!" She commented.

George Clemente shrugged. "What can I say? For some reason the local people prefer to use the cafe when we are not here."

"I understand that you have been given a contract for my friends here!" She indicated Donny and Abby.

"We do not discuss business here in the cafe." Eric broke in sharply.

George lifted his hand. "Isobel is our friend," he said quietly. "In answer to your query, yes, we have such a contract, but we did not know at the time that they were friends of yours. Had we known we would, of course have refused the contract. As it is..." he shrugged.

Isobel nodded with a sigh. "I'm sorry, losing friends is so upsetting. Can I persuade you perhaps?" This last was in a wistful voice, though she knew the answer even as she spoke."

She rose to her feet. "Come."She said to her friends. "Time we made a move." She turned to the Clemente brothers who had both risen to their feet. "George, Eric, I feel we will not meet again. Goodbye to you both; good luck."

Both killers kissed her hand and seemed genuinely upset at the thought of losing a friend. They waved farewell to the others. Aristide's face appeared briefly at the window as they drove off.

As they left Isobel said, "Know your enemy. Those two will be planning as we speak. They are extremely successful. There will be little chance of any mistakes in their planning. Our survival will depend on our own reactions, and our anticipation of what they have planned for us."

"You think they will carry out the contract if they can?" Abby said sadly.

"Their code of honour demands it. Having accepted the contract they must carry it out. They will do their best to make it as painless as possible, a swift clean death, if you see what I mean?"

"Thanks!" Adam said. "That will be a relief as I face the bullet!"

"Don't be absurd, Adam. You know as well as I that we will not allow that to happen. My sorrow at parting was for them not, us!"

Donny said, "I think that was what they were thinking. At least George was thinking. Eric seemed to think otherwise."

"He would. Unlike George, Eric is inclined to be rash, George keeps him at ground level most of the time. Now what I have in mind is the removal of friend Cortes. Initially that will slow things down. His current number-two is the man you caught in England as Cortes. He is a follower rather than leader. Alicia was obviously the greater loss to him than either his man, Albert, or Arturo Massa, the surrogate Cortes."

"What about the Brussels pair?"

"We leave them to Jonathon!" Donny said. "It is better that the law takes care of them, unless, of course, the law fails in its duty." He left the rest unsaid. There was no thought of sparing the pair retribution, however far removed they were from the actual kidnapping and the exploitation of the young people. In his eyes, they were as guilty as any of the others involved.

"So what we are left with is the man himself and the two killers. My suggestion is that if the boss Cortes is countered, the Clemente brothers may withdraw into the woodwork."

Isobel was just coming back into the room when mention was made of this. "You really must not even consider that will happen. It is their pride that they have never failed to carry out a commission. Depend on it, they will try, and it is in our interest not to forget it."

There was a period of silence after these words as the others all took them in.

***

Florien reported that the old school was being evacuated, not by the World Children's Charity, but by Cortes and his particular section. Jonathon had sifted through the paperwork recovered from the last activities there. Though there were indications of unorthodox events in the conduct of the Charity, there had been nothing that could be used to pin down Cortes or his staff in anything overtly illegal. The information about Cortes's boss he kept between Florien and himself.

***

The new offices were located temporally in two empty, summer-let cottages until more permanent quarters could be found. The cottages were available for three months and there was space for the accommodation of the defensive screen recruited by Cortes to ensure the operation was kept secure. With the discreet use of the tracer, the new location was found and Florien was able to re-establish surveillance almost immediately.

On the fringe of the Bois de Boulogne, a mere three minutes from Port Dauphine, the two cottages might have been in another world, remote from the bustle of the city. Located on the shores of the Lac Inferieur, there was easy access to the park and woodland, stretching west from the waterside. With the huge area of forest and park there was no real problem for the security arrangements installed by Cortes.

"This has been set up mainly with people armed with an odd assortment of weaponry, loosely scattered throughout the surrounding area, and supervised by Massa. There are trip wires and the odd booby trap." Florien Remy stood in front of the map of the Bois, using a pointer to indicate the cottages and the disposition of the men detailed to protect them. He put crosses where he knew trip wires and booby traps had been set-up. "I cannot be more specific as we are looking at uncharted areas more or less measured by eye while watchers were all about. Most of the men seem to be Parisians, though there are a couple of ex-soldiers amongst them.

The city dwellers looked not too keen on being dumped into the woods."

"How many are we up against?" Abby asked.

"Eight! Though that did include Massa." Florien said.

"Eight, and there is only four of us." Adam said.

"Five!" Florien interjected.

"Sorry. Five of us," he nodded in acknowledgement to Florien. "Not the worst odds we have faced. Is there anyone else we can bring in?"

"We do not really have time," Donny said. "We really have to act before they get settled properly. By the time Jonathon gets here it will be daylight." He was interrupted by a knock at the door. The entire party tensed up and all produced weapons. "I'll get it," Adam said, and made his way to the front door. Standing to one side he opened the door, gun up and ready.

John Bicycle stood there with a long bag hanging from his shoulder. "I have message from Jonathon, He will return direct to the Chateau. He sent me along to give you a hand. He should have arrived by now, so give him a ring, just in case!"

Donny looked at Adam. "Evens up the odds a little?"

Abby was speaking on the phone as the others greeted John.

Obviously pleased to be welcomed by the group, he opened his bag and uncovered the automatic shotgun he had acquired at the Chateau and proceeded to load it, ready for action.

Florien briefed John on the target. At 0100 hrs, they set-off for the Bois de Boulogne and the next phase of the operation.

Jonathon had arrived at the Chateau, having returned from a meeting in London. Abby put the phone down and reported that all was well there and that Jonathon had tried to stir some action up from his European colleagues without success.

Nathan Arquette turned the engine off and studied the impressive structure of the Chateau with interest. He could not see Jonathon's car because the lights had gone out. There were several lights shining from windows on the second story though little sign of life elsewhere. He switched off the interior light and opened the car door. Stepping out he closed the door quietly and started to skirt the gravel drive, walking on the grass toward the massive building.

The roads that run through the Bois de Boulogne are fairly busy during the day, but apart from the Peripherique, the ring road, most of the other roads quieten down overnight.

The two cars carrying the raiding party parked at Muette and they split up at that point, with an arranged rendezvous for regrouping after the raid.

Donny and Abby paired up, as did Isobel and Adam, both teams accustomed to working together. Florien and John comfortably teamed up and took their place in the line as they set off for the vicinity of the cottages. Florien had his crossbow. Having practiced, he was now quite expert at loading and his accuracy had improved to the level of 'deadly', as Adam put it.

Everyone switched cell phones to vibrate and they all disappeared into the shadows of the woodlands. The watcher where the team of Florien and John were operating had no chance at all. One moment he was having a quiet ciga-rette carefully shielded by his hand, the next he was dead. The Ingram smg dropped from his hand as he sank to the ground with a sigh. The bolt unheard, the pair unseen. Florien slung the Ingram over his shoulder. The pair moved on following the route already planned by him when he was watching the defenders setting up.

On the other side of the cottages Adam rose silently behind a watcher and circled his neck with his left arm. His right hand came round from the other side. While the startled man was still wondering, his head was turned with a jerk. The crack that followed signalled his loss of interest in the situation.

Adam lowered the dead man to the ground and removed the smg from his victim, passing it to Isobel who was crouched in the shadow behind him.

Donny and Abby had a clear run to within twenty feet of the near cottage. They found a trip wire. Abby followed it to the booby trap which was a simple grenade, the wire tied to the retaining pin. She removed the grenade and, making sure the pin was firmly home, she stuck it in her pack for future use.

She returned to Donny's side just as he encountered their first real opponent. The man walked out between two of the larger trees and was as surprised as Donny. Unfortunately for him he was not as quick to react. Donny's suppressed Walther PPK spoke while the man was still cocking his smg. The man crumpled looking hurt. Neither recognised him. They dragged the body off the path and hid it the bushes. The loose dust covered the blood.

Florien and John reached the wall of the near cottage before the others. John looked through the window. There was a man inside standing beside a table talking to another person who was out of sight. A TV was on in the corner of the room, but there was nothing else of interest. John made way for Florien to take a look.

After a few moments Florien shook his head, he did not recognize the man. Suddenly the man moved, startled. He made a grab for something that was not in Florien's view, but stopped and put his hands up. Florien turned back and tapped John on the shoulder. He moved around the corner of the building and, followed by John, went along the rear wall to the next corner. He stopped and listened. Dropping to his knees he peered round the corner. A big man, with a heavy weapon, was stepping up to the open door. In the small amount of reflected light it was possible for Florien to see the gleam of the man's teeth as he smiled.

With one smooth movement Florien brought up the crossbow and fired. At that short range he couldn't miss. The bolt took the man in the neck and passed right through tearing a ghastly wound that nearly severed his head from his shoulders. Florien stepped forward and caught the falling gun from the dead man's hands. He was retching, feeling sick at the sight of what the small crossbow could do. It was only the thought of what the gun weighing heavy in his hands, could have done to his friends that kept things together for him.

"Oh, god." Isobel was standing in the doorway having heard the big man fall. She could see the gaping wound in the man's neck. She saw Florien holding the big gun and her eyes widened. "Is that the gun he was carrying?" She nodded at the weapon. Florien managed to speak. "Yes, I saw him with this. He was smiling. I had to shoot him."

"Thank you, Florien. If he had fired at us with that thing, you would have needed a Hoover to gather us up for burial. Thank god you were there and acted fast." She stepped forward and gave him a hug.

"Let's get on with things. There are more people to find yet. Are you okay?"

Strangely, Florien felt much better. "I am now!" He said. "Much better."

The gun was a 12 bore automatic shotgun with an underslung grenade launcher. There were re-loads in a bandoleer over the man's shoulder. So stifling his disgust, Florien retrieved it and slung it round his own shoulder. He hung the crossbow on his belt and the two teams split up to support the attack on the other cottage.

Donny and Abby were nearly up to the other cottage when the second booby trap was found. Adam was in advance of Isobel and it was luck that allowed him to disarm the trap. It had been set up in a hurry and the trip wire was too long. Adam stepped on the wire and realized immediately what it was. He called Isobel forward. She came and held the wire in position while Adam followed it to the bomb. He did the same as Abby, disarming the bomb by replacing the pin, which was nearly entirely free. Having pushed it back in position he hooked it to his weapon belt.

Florien and John encountered opposition on the other side of the second cottage. The roar of the two shotguns woke the entire population of creatures in the woods. Three men died but Florien received a wound where a bullet creased his shoulder. It looked worse than it actually was. He appeared at the cottage leaning on John's shoulder.

Donny and Abby, had now been joined by Adam and Isobel, and Florien and John.

"No more creeping about. Let's go in and sort things out.

Adam kicked the front door in and a burst of shots came from within the cottage. Abby took out her grenade, lifted an eyebrow at Donny, pulled out the pin and rolled the bomb into the cottage. The blast shattered the inner door and to some extent the walls on each side, Screams echoed from within the building. Adam ignored them and sent his grenade in after the other, this time through the inner door. More screams followed the second explosion.

First through the door, Donny and Adam were closely followed by Abby and Isobel. Florien and John waited, keeping an eye on the woods around the area and listening for any sirens, just in case the police were going to appear.

Inside the cottage the place was trashed. The grenades had shattered the flimsy walls and the two people lying wounded were in a bad state. As Donny went through the doorway low and fast, two shots were fired. Both missed. Fired high, they hit the broken door jamb, and scattered splinters in a shower, causing Adam to duck. Donny, on the other side of the room, was firing at the point where Cortes lay behind the shelter of the old fashioned dresser.

Between the guns of Donny and Adam, Cortes did not have a chance. The gun battle was soon over. The position he was in exposed him to either Donny or Adam, whenever he tried to fire at either of them. They did not know whose bullet killed him. When he died, the survivor gave up and threw his gun out before rising with raised hands.

Donny's call to Jonathon was quick and brief. Jonathon put the call on speakerphone so that Marianne and the three girls could hear the news. Unbeknown to them all, Nathan Arquette also heard the news, from outside the window. He thought for a few moments, then as silently as he had arrived, he left. Jonathon did not realize how close he came to being killed.

The Bois raiders withdrew from the area. Copies of significant documents had been taken so that there would be no question of them being misplaced.

Isobel treated Florien's wound and he slept that night on cushions on the floor of their apartment. John had returned to the Chateau directly, to relieve Jonathon and allow him to step in with the official enquiry into the shoot–out in the Bois de Boulogne.

Over the next few days the four friends, with Florien, kept close to home, reminded by Isobel that the Clemence brothers were still out there, unlikely to give-up.

For Florien, the cross-bow had become a problem. However much he accepted that his shot had saved the lives of his friends, the picture of the devastation done by his bolt to the big man stayed with him. He sat on the flat roof outside the lounge window and cleaned the weapon. He wiped the remaining bolts with an oily rag, placing them back into the hard quiver, where each sat separately in their slot. He could hear the drowsy murmur of voices as the others chatted together.

The click of a hammer being pulled back took his immediate attention. It was unmistakeable. The voice was respectful, but hard. "Move aside, Isobel. You are not in the contract."

"Where is your brother, Eric? Does he know you are here?"

"He said the contract was discharged because the contractor was dead. I told him, just as I have told him before. A contract is a contract. If we are paid, we must perform. It is simple. Now move."

"You will have to shoot through me, and that will upset George," Isobel said reasonably.

"You do not understand. George is dead. He refused to listen, so I shot him. There has to be a proper system followed or there will be chaos. Now move."

Florien had moved until he could see without being seen, his fingers busy loading the crossbow.

Eric Clemente stood with his arm extended, gun in hand facing the four seated people. Isobel was standing between the gun and Abby, facing Eric determinedly.

Without thinking about it, Florien lifted the crossbow and shot Eric. The bolt went under the raised arm and passed between two ribs tearing lung and heart as it passed through.

Eric, for an instant, realized his fate but his finger could not press the trigger. He was no longer aware as he collapsed as if his bones had lost their rigidity.

The four in the room let out their respective breaths and relaxed. Then as one they turned on

Florien standing anxiously in the window, and swept him up between them.

***

Donny and Abby were back in Hillingdon. They had been back at the University for three days now and the events of the past weeks seemed to have happened in another life.

Jonathon called in to see them to confirm the success of the mission. He carried the good wishes of Florien and John, were still employed in the M16 information network. Florien and Grace his sister were both in process of becoming British citizens. She was still nanny to the Glynn family.

Jonathon carried cheques for Abby and Donny in payment for their period of employment as temporary agents for M16. He produced them with a flourish. "From a grateful Government," he said.

"No back pay for past services then?" Abby asked innocently.

***

In a Paris apartment Nathan Arquette, sat in a dark room, brooding.

..........the End?

David O'Neil

~*~*~

Other titles in O'Neil's Abby Marshall and Donny
Weston thriller series:
*****A Thrill a Minute*****
*****Fatal Meeting*****
*****Just One Thing After Another*****
*****Lethal Complications*****

~*~*~

Titles in O'Neil's Counterstroke series
*****Exciting, Isn't It?*****
*****Market Forces*****

~*~*~

Other adventure books by David O'Neil
*****The Mercy Run*****

David O'Neil

All titles available on line, at better book stores or at A-Argus Better Book Publishers. Also available in ebook form.

www.a-argusbooks.com